"What's going on? Who are you really?"

Nick's face was stoic. His jaw set. Determination creased his forehead now dark with ash. "You're in serious trouble."

"Start talking or I'm going to scream." She crossed her arms over her chest. "Or, better yet, take me home."

"No can do. And you needed help."

"Damn it, Nick, you're creeping me out. You have to give me something more." She didn't know why he'd shown up. Nothing made sense. "At least tell me where you're taking me. I deserve to know what's happening."

He kept one eye trained on the rearview mirror as he reached in his pocket and pulled out a badge. "I'm a US Marshal."

All those times he'd stopped in the bakery and led her to believe he was flirting with her caused a red blush to crawl up her neck. A piece of her had enjoyed his attention, too. What an idiot. Was he monitoring her situation the whole time? "You're a radiologist."

His lips parted in a dry crack of a smile. "You don't believe me."

"Why didn't you mention this before?"

"It would've blown my cover."

WITNESS PROTECTION

—

BARB HAN

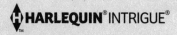

My deepest gratitude goes to the men and women of the US Marshals
Service for their many sacrifices. A heartfelt thank-you to my editor,
Allison Lyons, and my agent, Jill Marsal, because you make dreams
come true. I'm still pinching myself. Brandon, Jacob and Tori,
you guys inspire me every day. I love you with all my heart.
To my husband, John, you are the great love of my life.
And this is one heck of an adventure.

ISBN-13: 978-0-373-69804-2

Witness Protection

Copyright © 2014 by Barb Han

Recycling programs
for this product may
not exist in your area.

Printed in U.S.A.

ABOUT THE AUTHOR

Barb Han lives in North Texas with her very own hero-worthy husband, has three beautiful children, a spunky golden retriever/standard poodle mix and too many books in her to-read pile. In her downtime, she plays video games and spends much of her time on or around a basketball court. She's passionate about travel, and many of the places she visits end up in her books.

She loves interacting with readers and is grateful for their support. You can reach her at www.barbhan.com.

Books by Barb Han

1477—RANCHER RESCUE
1537—WITNESS PROTECTION*

*The Campbells of Creek Bend

CAST OF CHARACTERS

Sadie Brooks—She had to ditch her former life to enter Witness Protection. Now that the man she helped put behind bars has escaped, she'll walk away from another place, and the life she was finally building in Creek Bend. She must figure out a way to trust the man who shows up to help, even if doing so makes her more vulnerable.

Nick Campbell—This US Marshal, disguised as a nerdy work-at-home radiologist, shows up just in time to save Sadie from the criminal element who are close behind. But getting her to trust him is the tricky part, especially when his own past haunts him.

Luke Campbell—This FBI agent's blood ties mean he will do whatever it takes to help Nick and Sadie.

Charlie—The US Marshal assigned to be Sadie's handler turns up dead. Did he turn on her and give up her information to the criminal she put behind bars?

Malcom Grimes—This criminal has connections.

Deputy Jamison—The US Marshal supervisor's name keeps coming up in connection with Sadie's case.

William Smith—Nick's boss and mentor is helping call the shots.

Burly—The lethal henchman of a hardened criminal who will stop at nothing to make sure Sadie's life is erased.

Steroids—Another lethal henchman whose job is to track down and kill Sadie.

Chapter One

A clink against the back door of the bakery sounded again. Sadie Brooks lost her grip on the twenty-five pound sack of flour she'd held. It struck the floor and a mushroom-shaped cloud of white powder formed over the bag's lip.

Creek Bend, Texas, was a far cry from Chicago, she reminded herself. No one from her past knew where she was. No one could hurt her. No one cared. And she was no longer Laura Kaye.

It was four-thirty in the morning in a town that rolled up the streets by eight. The noise was most likely a cat rummaging through trash. No big deal. Nothing scary.

"Only you and me are crazy enough to be up this early," she said to her two-year-old rescue dog, Boomer, while forcing air in and out of her lungs. He didn't so much as crack an eyelid. "And I think we both know I mean me."

Working when everyone else slept suited Sadie just fine. She'd had very little use for daylight or people ever since she'd been kidnapped two years ago.

Yes, she still flinched at every noise. Constantly checked over her shoulder at the slightest peep. But she was always ready. Always expecting the worst. Always on guard. And yet, the past year had been peaceful. There was no reason to believe anything would change save for the all-too-real feeling in the pit of her stomach screaming otherwise.

Being constantly on alert felt a lot like parking and then leaving her high beams on. Pretty soon her battery would run out.

Boomer whined in his sleep. Her protector? Now that was funny. She'd rescued a big dog for protection. She got the Scooby Doo of golden retrievers. All he wanted to do was eat, and he wouldn't scare away a cat. But he did make noise and his low-belly bark sounded fierce. Sadie figured it was good enough to make anyone think twice.

As she bent over to pick up the sack of white powder, another noise sent a chill skittering across her nerves. Boomer's head cocked at the unmistakable snick of a lock. Her heart drummed against her chest.

Using the lock was good, right? That meant someone with a key was most likely standing on the other side of the door. She thought of Claire, her very pregnant boss who was her only friend. With her baby due any day, she would be asleep right now.

Boomer, shackles raised, stalked toward the stockroom to investigate.

"It's okay, boy." She scoured the area looking for a weapon just in case. Was there anything she could use to defend herself? To protect Boomer? She moved toward the nearest counter.

A sparkle caught her attention. Light reflected from the blade of a knife. Her fingers shook as they curled around the black plastic handle.

Then everything went dark. No lights. It was too much of a coincidence to think the breaker could've been tripped. This blackout was on purpose.

Boomer's low throaty growl nearly stopped her heart. It

was the same noise he made when a stranger approached the lake house. Boomer had found an intruder. And they weren't familiar.

His barks fired like a machine gun, rapid and ear-piercing.

Sadie's adrenaline kicked into high gear. Her fight, flight or freeze response jacked through the roof. Every instinct inside her screamed, "Run!"

But she couldn't.

She wouldn't leave Boomer defenseless. Could she signal to him without giving away her location? No.

What about help? Her cell? Good luck finding her purse in the pitch-black.

She crouched and felt her way behind a rack filled with pastries. A hand covered her mouth. Her fingers, which had been curled around the knife handle, flexed cold air. She had been disarmed with frightening ease.

"Shh. Don't say a word or they'll hear you. Be very still." A second ticked by before she recognized the voice as Nick Campbell's. Why in the hell would a radiologist show up at the bakery in the middle of the night?

The last time a man took her by surprise she ended up spending two weeks in the ICU with facial lacerations and cracked ribs.

Determined to break free this time, she ignored the shivers running up her arms and bit Nick's hand.

"I said, 'be still,' and don't do that again," Nick said. His deep, quiet tone was different. Dark and dangerous. Experienced. And she knew instinctively not to push him.

With a total stranger somewhere in front of her and Nick's big frame behind her, she was trapped.

"I won't hurt you," he whispered.

What on earth was he doing here? And how had he gotten in without her noticing?

Boomer's barks mixed with growls and intensified.

Before she could wrap her brain around what was happening, Sadie felt herself being hauled toward the front door. The recollection of being snatched in daylight two years ago flooded her. His behavior brought up horrible memories. No way would Nick Campbell abduct her. Not a chance.

But what, besides a feeling that she could trust him, did she know about Nick? His brown eyes and black hair were almost always covered by a ball cap and shades. His shoulders hunkered forward, masking his true height. She hadn't fully realized his lethal potential until he stood behind her, his masculine chest flush with her back. She was five-foot-seven and he dwarfed her. He had to be more than six feet tall. Maybe six-one?

Neither his height nor his mannerisms had intimidated her before. She'd felt a sizzle of attraction, but then most of the women in Creek Bend seemed eager to get to know him better. With his forearm locked like a vise grip around her waist, she suddenly realized just how strong and buff he truly was.

"What do you think you're doing?" she whispered, choking down the anger rising inside her.

"No time to explain."

Hell if she'd wait. She wasn't about to be caught with no means of self-preservation again. She wasn't defenseless as she'd been before.

The first principle of judo was never to oppose strength to strength. Sadie shifted her weight enough to kick off the wall. She bucked, trying to throw him off balance while bracing herself to land on the painted concrete floor.

Didn't work.

Strong as an ox, he'd anticipated the move and counteracted by placing his feet in an athletic stance and tightening his grip. "I'll drag you out of here kicking and screaming if I have to, but we'll most likely both be killed."

"I can't leave my dog. Boomer's back there," she said, hating how her voice quivered and got all shaky with fear. She'd sworn no man would make her feel defenseless again. She realized, on some level, he was there to help, but she could walk for herself.

She kicked and wiggled. His grip was too tight.

It surprised her that a nerdy work-at-home radiologist knew how to counteract her martial arts moves. He also knew the back of the bakery well enough to navigate in the dark. She couldn't even do that without bumping into something and she'd worked there for a year.

Fighting was no use. She would bide her time and break free the second the opportunity presented.

"I'll go back for him. Once you're safe in the truck," he said. "Trust me."

She snorted. "Why? Because I know so much about you?"

"I can explain everything. Once you're out of danger."

Bright Christmas lights lit a cloudless sky. Once they were out of the building, she could see. Nick's expression was that of soldier on the front line.

He tucked her in the truck and then closed the door. The lock clicked. Trust him?

The door handle didn't work. She rammed the door. All that did was hurt her shoulder. Try again and there'd be a nasty bruise. There had to be another way. She banged on the window. "Hey!"

She tried to pop the lock. Nothing.

Spinning onto her back, she used a front kick to drive

the heel of her foot into the door, praying she could find the sweet spot. No good.

She scrambled to the front seat. By the time she gripped the handle, she heard a horrific boom from the alley. The bakery caught fire. She couldn't catch her breath enough to scream.

The world closed in around her, and her stomach wrenched. Boomer!

Shattered glass littered the sidewalk. Thick black smoke bellowed from every opening.

What was left of the front door kicked open and out strode Nick, coughing, with her hundred-pound mutt in his arms.

As soon as she got a good look at him saving her dog, her heart squeezed and a voice inside her head warned, *Uh-oh.*

Out of the ashes and burning timber, he moved toward her, carrying her dog as if Boomer weighed nothing. Nick opened the back door of the truck and gently placed the dog on the seat.

"What's going on? Who are you really?"

There was something about his compassion with the animal, something nonthreatening about him that kept Sadie's nerves a notch below panic.

His face was stoic. His jaw set. Determination creased his forehead now dark with ash. "You're in serious trouble."

Icy tendrils closed around her chest. "What are you doing here showing up out of nowhere like that? Who was coming in the back door?"

He started the ignition.

"Start talking or I'm going to scream." She crossed her arms over her chest. "Or, better yet, take me home."

"No can do. And you needed help."

"Dammit, Nick, you're creeping me out. You have to give me something more."

His determination was written all over his squared jaw. He had obviously saved her life. He wasn't there to hurt her. She didn't know why he'd shown up. Nothing made sense. "At least tell me where you're taking me. I deserve to know what's happening."

He kept one eye trained on the rearview mirror as he reached in his pocket and pulled out a badge. "I'm a U.S. Marshal."

Her brain scrambled. Where was Charlie? He was her handler. And what did Nick mean he was a U.S. Marshal? All those times he'd stopped in the bakery and led her to believe he was flirting with her caused a red blush to crawl up her neck. A piece of her had enjoyed his attention, too. What an idiot. Was he monitoring her situation the whole time? She needed to call Charlie and find out what was going on. For now, it was best to ignore her embarrassment and play dumb. "You're a radiologist."

His lips parted in a dry crack of a smile. "You don't believe me."

"Why didn't you mention this before?"

"It would've blown my cover."

ANGER FLASHED IN Sadie's big green eyes as her gaze darted around the vehicle. Her phone was her only connection to her handler, and it was just as lost as she looked. She turned her attention to him, glaring as if this was all his fault.

"Sorry about your cell." He pulled a new one from the dash and handed it to her. The movement called attention to the bruise she'd put on the inside of his forearm when she'd tried to kick out of his grasp earlier. The memory of her slim figure and sweet bottom pressed against him stirred an inappropriate sexual reaction. Her flour-dotted pale pink V-neck sweater and jeans fit like a second skin over a toned, feminine body. Her fresh-baked-bread-and-lily scent filled the cab. "I didn't have time to retrieve your purse."

She looked at the phone as if it was a hot grenade. "Why should I trust you?"

Nick couldn't blame her. Her world was about to be turned upside down again, and he sensed she knew on some level. "You don't have a choice. I apologize for that."

She recoiled, most likely remembering being forced away from the only life she'd known in Chicago two years ago. His surveillance told him she'd made a home in Creek Bend and a friend in her new boss. The two had become close. Claire and her baby were a surrogate family to Sadie. He didn't like taking it all away again. He bit back frustration.

"Where are you taking me?" The fear in her voice was like a sucker punch to his solar plexus.

"Somewhere safe. Charlie's dead."

She gasped. Her shaky hand covered her mouth.

"How do you know? Did you…?"

"No. Of course not." She'd been taught not to believe anyone but Charlie. He had no idea how she would react now. He'd have to keep a close eye on her during the ride. "I know this is a lot to digest."

She sat there tight-lipped, looking as though she'd bolt if given the chance.

"This is real. You're in danger. I'm here to help."

Her angry glare trained on him. "Prove he's dead."

"Can't. Not tonight, anyway."

"Why? Shouldn't there be a news report? A U.S. Marshal dying should make the headlines."

"It's complicated."

"Then explain it to me slowly." She clenched her jaw muscles. Impatience and fear radiated from her narrow-eyed glare.

With her wavy brown hair pulled off her face in a ponytail, she could pass for a coed. Her lips were full, sexy. Not that they were his business. "He was found in his bed. A bullet through his brain. The agency is keeping his death under wraps."

"Oh, God. He was a nice man."

Nick bit out a derisive snort. "Good guys don't get in bed with the enemy."

"Are you saying what I think you are?" she asked incredulously.

"Yes, ma'am."

"I don't believe you. He brought me here. Set me up with this job. He would not help them."

He arched his brow. "Because he did a few nice things for you, he can't possibly turn into one of them?"

She stared at the road in front of them. If she bit down any harder on her bottom lip, she might chew right through it. "Don't twist my words. I know he was a family man. He cared about his work. I knew him better than you did. He wouldn't turn on me. Not now. Not after two years. Besides, what would he have to gain in hurting me?"

"Malcolm Grimes has been broken out of jail and someone on the inside helped. Your handler showed up at the prison two days before he escaped."

Her tight grip on her nerves shattered. Just like when a rubber band broke, Nick could almost see the pieces of rubber splintering in all directions. Her eyes closed. Her fingers pressed to her temples. Her body visibly shook. "He's out? Just like that?"

"I'm afraid so."

Her eyes snapped open and her gaze locked on to him. "How can you let that happen? Now he's free to come after me?" Her voice shook with terror.

"That's why I'm here."

"Let me get this straight. Grimes is out, and you automatically suspect Charlie? Wouldn't he be alive right now if he'd helped?"

"Not if he crossed Grimes. He was executed in his own bed. Someone was making a statement."

Weariness crept over her face as she gripped the phone, closed her eyes again and rocked back in her seat. "The first thing Grimes does after killing Charlie is come after me? Why? Wouldn't he figure you'd be waiting for him?"

"Your file's missing from Charlie's place."

She drummed her index finger on the cell.

"I'm supposed to tell you 'Pandora.'"

The tension in her face eased slightly even though she didn't speak. Her movement smoothed, timed with her calmer breaths. She stopped tapping on the cell. The safe word resonated. "Any idea why my boss chose Pandora as your safe word?"

"Yeah."

"Care to fill me in?" It wasn't as if he was asking for her Social Security number.

"Not really." A solemn expression settled on her almond-shaped face. "The bakery. Did they blow it up because of me?"

"Most likely."

"That was all Claire had to support her baby and now it's gone. Why didn't they just shoot me straight out?"

He tightened his grip on the steering wheel. "Good question. My guess is they were trying to ensure there'd be no mistakes. Easier to just blow up a building with you in it. Also has the added benefit of looking like it was an accident. It's tidier. Leaves less of a trail."

"So, it's over. Just like that. I walk away from everything I know one more time because of these jerks. I'm on the move again?"

He nodded.

"I didn't do anything wrong," she said fiercely.

"I know."

"Is this what I can expect the rest of my life? Because some guys want to murder and maim me?" She drummed her hands on the dash. Her tension was on the rise again.

"It shouldn't happen to good people."

"Save the speech. I've heard it before. 'Nice folks deserve better than this, but we have to do what we can to protect you. It's not your fault. Sometimes the system doesn't work.'"

"It's true."

She pressed her lips together. "Yeah? Well, your system sucks."

He could appreciate her anger. When his youngest sister was kidnapped and beaten by a crazed ex-boyfriend, Nick had hunted the teen down and nearly ended up in prison himself. His mom intervened while his grandmother called 911 to stop him from meting out his own justice. Sadie's haunted expression reminded him of his kid sister.

Under the circumstances, Sadie was doing well. Damn that his own anger rose thinking about the past. He already felt a connection to Sadie. His protective instincts flew into high gear the moment someone breached the bakery. He shouldn't care this much about a witness. "It'll keep you alive if you let it."

A beat of silence sat between them.

He risked a glance in her direction. A ball of fury formed in his throat at the tears streaming down her pink cheeks. From what he'd observed in the few weeks he'd been in Creek Bend, she worked hard. She was always on time. By all accounts she did a great job. He already knew about her resilience and courage. She seemed decent and kind. She deserved so much more.

He might have to take away her home again, but he would keep her safe.

Rather than debate the quality of the WitSec program at the U.S. Marshals Service, he dropped his defenses. The experience of growing up with four women under the same roof had taught him a thing or two about the point at which he'd lost a battle. He didn't need any of his experience to see this one was long gone. He raised his hands in the universal sign of surrender then dropped them right back on the steering wheel. "I didn't say any of that to upset you."

She folded her arms. "It's fine. I guess you're right. The program probably helps a lot of people. Just not me. I get to be the exception. I might be the unluckiest person on the planet. Even a program meant to help people makes my life miserable."

"For what it's worth, I'm truly sorry."

She looked at him long and hard. Her green-eyed stare pierced him. "Your boss, Mr. Smith, said whatever I stepped into opened a Pandora's box because they started fighting to take over Grimes's territory."

"Sounds like something my boss would say." He clenched his back teeth. "It did. Violent crime shot through the roof after we put Grimes away."

"Doesn't seem like I helped by having him locked away."

"Testifying was still the right thing to do. You saved a lot of innocent lives."

"Did I? Not mine. And what about Claire? Now I've ruined the business of the one person who I could count on as a friend."

"She'll receive money. I guarantee it. Citizens are safer with these guys off the streets."

"But they aren't, are they?" she snapped. "I wasn't even the one Grimes wanted. They kidnapped me by mistake. The woman they were after moved away and disappeared. She was smart. Not me. I believed your boss. I testified. Look at me now. Shouldn't you check in with him or something?" She palmed the cell, scrolling through the names in the contact list with her thumb.

It didn't take long.

There were only two. Nick Campbell. William Smith.

They were the only two people in her world for now. Nick couldn't imagine being that alone.

"Nah. There's only one reason I want you to call that number. Anything happens to me, don't hesitate. Make contact. Smith will tell you where to go and what to do."

Her grip tightened on the cell phone. "But you're with me. Anything happens to you and we'll both be dead."

"Nothing's going to happen to either of us. I promise. I only gave you the number to ease your concerns."

"If one U.S. Marshal's already dead, our odds don't seem all that great." Her words came out raspy and small.

The back windshield shattered. The truck swerved as he slammed the brakes.

A truck rammed his left bumper, sending his vehicle into a dangerous spin. He grasped the steering wheel, turning into the skid.

Chapter Two

Cold blasted Sadie. "Boomer!"

He'd never been good at car rides. She glanced in the backseat. He was practically plastered to the floor mat. His fear might've just saved his life.

"Get down." Nick's tone changed to a dark rumbling presence of its own.

Rocks and dirt spewed from under the tires as he navigated the vehicle back onto the roadway.

Sadie curled into a ball on the floorboard. "That the same person who was trying to get through the door at the bakery?"

"No."

She flashed her gaze toward him. "How do you know?"

Oh. Right. He'd killed him. The soot on his face outlined the scratches he'd collected. Looking at this guy—this new Nick—she believed him capable of doing whatever was necessary to get the job done. The transformation from the old one still shocked her. The once almost nerdy-looking facade a stark contrast to the battle-weary expression of this warrior. If he drove as well as he hid his identity, she had no doubt he'd get them out of this.

The truck swerved and jolted her thoughts to the very real threat screaming toward the back bumper.

The image of Nick calm and collected despite the danger brought her panic levels down.

He aimed a revolver out the back and fired a round.

The squeal of tires, the crunch of metal against a tree, and she knew another bad guy was dead.

Nick floored the gas pedal. He had the wheel in one hand and his weapon in the other.

An invisible band tightened around her rib cage.

Nick looked at her, his expression serious and reassuring. "We're okay."

"I know."

With one hand on the wheel and his eyes on the road, he placed the gun on the seat between them and offered a hand up. She pulled herself up onto the bench seat.

He turned the heater on high and then shrugged out of his leather jacket. "This should help."

She realizing for the first time her teeth were chattering. Wrapping the coat around her shoulders, she was flooded with the masculine scent of leather.

"I'm not going to let anyone hurt you." He was sweet to make the promise even if they both knew he didn't have control over what happened to her.

Even so, her heart rate slowed a notch. "Th-thank you."

With the gun next to her, prickly heat flushed her neck and face. An overwhelming fear pressed down on her body, making her limbs heavy.

Concern wrinkled his charred forehead. "What's wrong?" His gaze shifted from the firearm to her face then back to the road. "This? Does seeing my gun bother you?"

"It's okay. I have to get used to it, right? This is my life now." She heard how small her voice had become, hating that she'd lost her power by looking at the piece of cold metal.

"Not today." He slipped the weapon into an ankle holster and tugged his jeans over it.

She'd barely noticed his legs until that moment. Her gaze moved up to the line of his muscular thighs pressing against the denim material of his jeans. A black V-neck T-shirt highlighted a broad chest and arms as thick as tree trunks.

An electric current swirled inside her body. This strong man looked more than capable of protecting her. He seemed able to handle anything that came along. She realized why she'd never noticed how adept and strong he'd been before. There had been no reason to. He'd played the work-at-home radiologist to perfection. Most of the women in Creek Bend had noticed his seriously good looks and lucrative career, while she'd spent the past year trying to avoid everyone—especially men. She'd closed her eyes to anyone she'd dismissed as a nonthreat.

Odd as it sounded, she would miss seeing Nick come into the bakery right before her shift ended. Different didn't begin to describe the change in him. She'd already been introduced to his powerful chest and lean, muscled thighs when her body had been pressed against his earlier. Forget about his strong hands around her and the sensual current they had sent through her body.

This close, she could see his almost overwhelmingly attractive facial features. His brown eyes had cinnamon copperlike flecks in them. His jawline with two days' worth of stubble a sharp contrast to full, thick lips—lips she had to force her gaze away from. His dense, wavy hair was as black as his shirt. The combination made for one seriously hot package.

She thought about how fast the bakery had gone up

in flames. Her boss and only friend who had become like family would have to start over. Claire had worked hard to build her business. The building would be burned to the ground by now. A little piece of her broke at the thought of never seeing Claire's baby. Her only real friend was out of her life forever.

Friend? Sadie almost laughed out loud. What kind of friend didn't even know her real name?

A sign that read Now Leaving Creek Bend filled the right corner of the window.

She thought about the town Christmas party she wouldn't attend. About the baby she would never meet. About the family of her own that was so out of reach. About all the things she would never have.

Burning tears rolled down her cheeks.

A feeling of loss anchored in her stomach.

Straightening her back, she clicked on her seat belt. Let those bastards get inside her head, and they won. "There are a few knickknacks back home I wish I had." She glanced at her taupe boots with teal outlay and sighed. "At least I get to keep these."

Nick's gaze intensified on the road. "I already sent someone for your things."

"Seriously? Isn't that against the rules or something?"

He shrugged. "We'll keep 'em somewhere locked away until it's safe to retrieve them."

"I don't know what to say. That was very kind of you. I was told everything had to be left behind when this happens."

"It's not the way I work." His gaze intensified on the stretch of road in front of him. "You deserve to have your clothes at least."

Appreciation washed over her. She knew not to trust

it. "This is the second time I've thanked you since we've been in the truck."

Sadie forced herself to remember other positive things as she reached in the backseat to pet Boomer. Not losing everything was a huge blessing.

Besides, the alternative—giving up—was never an option. All she could gain there was depression. Feeling sorry for herself wouldn't change her circumstances. Alcohol? A drinking problem didn't sound like the worst demon to battle at the moment. But, no, she'd never really taken to the taste other than an occasional glass of wine.

She turned toward the stranger beside her as he pulled the truck off the main road. "Is Nick Campbell your real name?"

"Yes," he said with the voice that was like a caress on a cold winter's night. He arched his dark brow.

"Are you telling me the truth?"

"You deserve that much from me."

A traitorous shiver skittered across her nerves. It was chilly outside. Now that the window had shattered, there was nothing keeping out the frost. The shiver came from being cold, she told herself, and not the sexual appeal of the man next to her. "This can't be the work of Grimes alone, can it? Is he big enough to take out a U.S. Marshal?"

"It's stupid to come after you. The agency has been keeping a close eye on everything since his escape. Smith and I were hoping he'd leave you out of this. And, yes, there's more to this than we know as of now. But we'll figure the rest out."

"Doesn't sound good for me. Maybe he wants revenge badly enough to risk everything?"

"He didn't get where he is by being stupid."

"He's been out for a month? Timed with when you showed up?"

"We received intel something was brewing. My boss wanted to make sure our bases were covered. I came out a few days before he broke out."

The Christmas party invitation she'd received flashed in her mind. A small town holiday scene complete with four-foot-high snowdrifts piled on either side of the road. There were glowing street lamps. The scene reminded her very much of Creek Bend sans the snow. Sadie's boss had all but made her promise she'd show. "What would make him risk his safety to find me? He can't possibly want to go back to prison. I mean, why me? Why now?"

His jaw muscle ticked. "Revenge."

That one word packed more power than if she'd been struck with a fist. "I was upset before. I didn't mean to insult the agency. I honestly appreciate everything you guys have done to keep me alive so far."

"Our failures are putting your life at risk."

And keeping her on the run. Creek Bend would start its day perfectly timed to the sunrise in another forty-five minutes. Life would go on without her.

Claire would have her baby. Sadie would never hold the little girl she'd anticipated for so long. Claire had become more than a friend, she'd become like family. And now everything was gone.

At least she still had Boomer. He was tucked safely in the backseat. "None of this has ever made sense to me. I didn't do anything wrong and yet I'm the one slinking out of town in the middle of the night."

Sadie's sadness was palpable. Worse yet, she put up a brave front.

One look into those haltingly green eyes, transparent like single perfect gemstones, and Nick might forget his real reason for being there. Protect his witness without getting overly involved. Not generally a problem for him. Discipline was more than his middle name. It was his life's creed.

Nothing and no one had threatened his ability to focus. Or could.

This was different. Her circumstance reminded him too much of his little sister's. The thought of another woman being targeted by a man hell-bent on revenge when she was innocent ate at his insides. Many of the people in the program he came across could use a fresh start. Giving them a new job and home also provided a new lease on life. Not Sadie. What had she done wrong? Nothing. By all accounts, she should've had a promising future with a business consultant in accounting. She'd be well on her way to two-point-five kids, a big house and a Suburban.

None of *this* had been invited into her life. A crazed criminal had sent her to the ICU.

People called her lucky for living.

Luck wasn't her gig. She'd had enough courage to defy the odds and enough spunk to fight when her future was bleak.

What she had was a hell of a lot better than chance.

And yet, seeing her now, she looked small and afraid. Chin up, she was determined not to give into it.

He'd give anything to ease her concern and put a smile on her face. Wanting to protect her and needing to were two different things.

Why was he already reminding himself of the fact?

He pulled the truck onto a narrow dirt road. "I have better transportation stashed here. Besides, we won't make it five miles without drawing attention with the condition of the truck."

Winding down the lane wasn't a problem. Turning off the lights and navigating in the dark was a different story. He'd memorized the area easy enough. But he hadn't had time to make a night run.

A thunk sounded at the same time they both pitched forward. The air bags deployed. Sadie gasped and Boomer yelped as he banged against the back of the driver's seat.

"Hold on, boy," she said.

Nick focused on Sadie first. "You okay?"

"Fine."

He hopped out of the truck and opened the door to the backseat of the cab. Running a hand over the frightened dog, Nick didn't feel anything out of the ordinary. He checked his hand for blood. Relief was like a flood to dry plains. "Shook him up a bit."

She struggled to work herself free from the airbag, and then climbed over the seat. "But he's fine, right?"

"Yep." Nick owed the big guy upstairs one for that.

What caused the wreck? Had he misjudged the road?

He circled to the front of the cab. His eyes were adjusting to the dark. The sight before him pumped his stress level fifty notches. A tree blocked the road.

He seriously doubted nature had caused the barrier. Had someone found his hiding spot?

A branch snapped to his right. Could be an animal evading, but he wouldn't take unnecessary chances with his cargo. He moved to the truck. "We can't drive through. We'll have to go on foot."

Sadie nodded, coaxing Boomer to follow.

Nick shouldered his backpack. They had enough

supplies to last a couple of days. He hadn't expected to need them.

"Where're we going?" Sadie's eyes were wide and she blinked rapidly. Fear.

"There's a place about a day's hike from here. If we can make it by nightfall, we'll have safe shelter."

Her gaze locked on to the barrier behind them. "That wasn't an accident, was it?"

He shrugged his shoulders casually, not wanting her to panic. "I'd rather not take anything for granted."

The crack and crunch of tree limbs on the ground grew louder.

Boomer faced the woods on the opposite side of the truck. His shackles raised, and he growled low in his belly.

Nick reached for Sadie's hand, and then wound his fingers through hers.

"We have to go. *Now.*"

Chapter Three

Nick pulled Sadie into the woods at a dead run. Branches slapped her face and arms, stinging her skin.

Boomer quickened his stride, keeping pace by her side step for step.

They could've been banging drums for all the noise they made. No chance they'd slip through the brush unheard. Nick seemed more intent on moving fast. Another reason her pulse kicked up and her anxiety levels roared.

Her thighs hurt. Her lungs burned. She pushed forward, determined not to complain.

He stopped at the edge of a lake. She collapsed to the ground, gasping for air. Her ears were numb, frozen. Every other body part overheated.

Sunlight pushed through the trees, which meant they'd been on the go at least forty-five minutes. Her lungs felt as if they'd explode, whereas Nick hardly seemed affected. Of course he was in shape. His job—his *real* job—would demand excellent physical conditioning. She forced her gaze away from the way his muscles expanded against his jeans when he walked.

The rustle of leaves and bird whistles were the only noise. "Is it safe to take a break?"

He stood, listening. Then he scanned the area. "We can take a minute."

"What about the racket we made?"

"I made a few shortcuts that made it harder to track us." He opened his pack and handed her a bottle of water, taking one for himself. "Let me know when you think you can move again."

She could barely open the lid. Tired and dirty, her stamina waned. The cool liquid was a godsend to her parched mouth. "So what's the plan?"

"Shelter. But it's a ways ahead," he warned. "It isn't much, but it'll get us through the night."

"No. I mean ultimately. Where is all this hiding going? Surely no one expects me to keep this up forever."

"If you're tired we can stop."

"I don't mean now."

His face tensed. His glare intensified. His slack jaw became rigid.

"What? No answers?"

"You want the truth? We catch him, figure out who else is involved and why, and get your life back." He turned to face the lake.

"I doubt that," she huffed. "What good did it do me to testify? I never got my life back. His men kept searching for me. I've had two homes in two years. Now, he's out. Hunting me. I'm running for my life. Again. Your boss made promises he didn't keep."

Nick bent down and poured water on his palm, allowing Boomer a drink. When the dog was hydrated, Nick took a swig of water. "He shouldn't have done that."

"It was all well and good when people wanted me to help them." She pulled her knees into her chest. "I'm sure it didn't hurt his career to be able to put a man like Grimes away."

He whirled around on her. "What's that supposed to mean?"

"How much do you trust your boss?" Anger had her bating him into an argument.

"Smith is fine. You're tired."

"Is that right?"

"I hope so because if this is your personality, it's gonna be a long night."

"You think this is funny? Forgive me if I don't laugh along with you."

Nick cleared his throat. "I never said that. I'm not here to hurt you. In case you hadn't noticed, I'm trying to help."

"For how long? You can't watch me the rest of my life. Maybe I should go after him for a change." What she'd said was the emotional equivalent of raising a red blanket in front of a bull. She had two choices. Fight or cry. She'd rather fight.

"Now you're being crazy."

Tears welled, but she'd be damned if they were going to fall. "First I'm tired. Now I'm crazy. Which is it?"

"I get why you're…freaking out."

"Do you? You think you already know what's going on inside my head? Why don't you tell me, then, because I'm confused." She shot daggers at him with her glare. Fear pushed away the cold air, replacing it with heat. Her body vibrated from anger, her defense mechanism for not losing it and crying.

She stood and took a step toward him. She expected to see anger or confusion. Instead, he faced her with his whole body. His hands were open at his sides. His relaxed gaze moved smoothly from her eyes to her mouth and back. His lips softened at the corners in a smile.

She steeled her breath, but nothing prepared her for the warmth of his big hand on her shoulder.

The fight drained from her.

"We have a long walk ahead. You should save your energy."

Her chest deflated. She plopped onto the cold ground. Boomer nuzzled his cold wet nose on her neck.

"Give me a minute. I'll be fine."

THE LAST THING Sadie looked was fine. If he'd learned one thing from having two sisters, the word *fine* didn't mean good things. He'd give her a minute to regroup even though he'd feel a lot better if they kept moving. They'd put some distance between them and whoever was following, but for how long? "For what it's worth, my sisters tell me I'm stubborn. If I were in your situation, I'd be crazy, too."

She rewarded him with a smile warmer than a campfire. "Smart women."

"Don't tell them that." He bent down on his knee, fighting the urge to provide more comfort than his words.

"Do I detect a case of sibling rivalry?" Her brow arched.

"No. But I do have two younger sisters to keep track of."

"You must be exhausted."

"Not really. They can take care of themselves mostly. Both work in law enforcement. They humor me, though."

She relaxed a little more. "Bet I could learn a thing or two from them."

"I doubt it. You're a survivor."

"How do you know?"

"You've made it this far."

"You never told me where we're going. Do you have a hunting cabin or something out here?" she asked.

"Guess I didn't adequately fill you in. I'd apologize but I'll just do it again. My sisters tell me I tend to get in a zone then information comes out on a need-to-know basis."

"Does that mean your brain can act and speak at the same time?"

He laughed. "It's possible. Words are empty, though." He could hear his grandmother's voice in the back of his head echoing the same sentiment. "Actions are better."

She'd also taught him to be grateful for what he had instead of sorrowful for what he'd lost. Some lessons were easier to catch on to than others.

Sadie's laugh had the same effect as the first spring flower opening. "You've been surrounded by a lot of smart women in your life, haven't you? You're lucky."

"Not sure if you would hold on to that thought if you spent more than five minutes with them."

Her gaze focused on the water and she absently picked at a leaf. "I'm afraid I don't have a big family to draw experience from. It's just me. Has always been just me."

He nodded.

She glanced at him. "Right. You already knew that didn't you? You probably know everything about me, don't you?"

"The agency gave me your intel. For what it's worth—"

"Don't apologize. You'll just do it again when you need information about someone." She half smiled.

"True."

"I know you were doing your job. I'm not blaming you personally. It's just surreal to me that there's some file out there with my life history in it."

Silence sat between them.

"It's been me, alone, for so long, I can't remember what it's like to have a real family. It was just me and my parents growing up. I never had more than that. They were always working. I wouldn't know what to do with siblings who watch over me."

"A big family sounds like heaven in theory. In real life, not so much. Add my mom and grandmother into the mix and I've had four women constantly telling me what to do for most of my life." He chuckled.

"Sounds like the promised land to me right now."

"Mom had a lot of mouths to feed when my dad disappeared. She'd come home beat, but tried not to show it. I became a handful. My dad leaving didn't do good things to my head. But then I saw how much pain I added to my mom. She was already devastated. Being the oldest, I got a front-row seat to her pain."

"From the looks of it, you turned out okay."

"That's still up for debate."

"You're a U.S. Marshal. You change people's lives with your work. I'd be dead right now if not for you. I'm sure dozens of other people would say the same thing."

He tightened his grip on the water bottle as he screwed on the lid. "Think you can walk?"

"I'd like to hear more about your family." Her voice hitched on the word *family*. Was she thinking about his family, or the husband and kids she should already have with the accounting consultant in Chicago?

A twinge of jealousy heated his chest. He ignored it. "There isn't much else to tell. I have two brothers."

She rolled her eyes. "Are you focused again?"

He couldn't help but smile. "Not intentional. I'm thinking about getting us both through the night."

She straightened her back and glanced around. "Any chance they gave up and went home?"

"They've come this far. They won't stop looking."

"You said there's a place we can stay?"

He nodded.

"That the best idea? I mean, shouldn't we get out of here altogether? Maybe call for backup?"

"Afraid we're on our own this time." A warm sensation surged through him when he thought about the implication of being alone with her in the small cabin all night. One bed.

She turned and his gaze drifted down the curve of her back to her sweet bottom. Another time, different circumstances, he could think of dozens of things he'd like to do with her on that bed. This wasn't the time for inappropriate sexual fantasies.

"Why are we on our own?"

"Smith made the call. I agree. Can't risk anyone on the inside knowing your status or whereabouts in case there's a leak. We have to consider the fact this might be bigger than Charlie."

"How many people in the agency know about me?"

"Now?"

She nodded.

"As far as we know, me and Smith. We'd like to keep it that way."

"Then what are you afraid of?"

"If Grimes found a way in with Charlie, I wonder what other connections he made. We think we're the only two with your intel, but we can't be sure. Your file was with Charlie. Now it's missing. Did he tell anyone else about you before he was killed? We have no clue. There's too much uncertainty."

"I know what they did to me, but what other crimes are they responsible for?"

"Grimes is well-connected. Has his hands in contract

killings, loan sharking, gambling, bribery—to name a few. His channels run from South America to Canada, and straight through Chicago."

"Sounds big-time."

"Ever play the game Six Degrees of Separation?" He looked at her.

"Yeah. Sure. Why?"

"He's the Kevin Bacon of crime."

She shifted her weight and looked at him. "Or he was…"

"Until you put him away, which started a war. Now that he's out, we have no idea what to expect."

"Pandora's box?"

"Armageddon."

"Still doesn't explain what he wants with me. Except good old-fashioned revenge, I guess." Sadie stood and wiped the dried leaves clinging to the back of her jeans.

"He's not exactly a nice guy. He's capable of doing a lot of damage on his own. We can't underestimate him or his connections."

"Lucky me."

Nick closed the water bottles, zipped the pack and shouldered it. The winds had picked up and the air had a cold bite. "We'll catch him. Or the marshals, or the feds will."

"You believe that, don't you?"

"It's my job. The system isn't perfect. Sometimes it fails. I see it succeed ninety-nine percent of the time."

She stared at him incredulously. "You don't need to tell me about the system. I'm living proof it doesn't work."

Nick didn't offer a defense. Sadie was the exception. He inclined his chin and powered forward.

The best thing he could do for her was give her a half-decent night of sleep in a comfortable bed. A hot shower and warm bowl of soup would defrost her and revive her energy.

"You good at what you do?"

"The best."

"Excellent. I wouldn't want to be stuck out here with an amateur." She turned and made kissing noises at Boomer, who dutifully followed.

Nick kept a brisk pace until they reached the small cabin before dark, only stopping long enough to eat a Power Bar for lunch. Sadie followed close behind; the crunch of tree branches under her boots and her labored breathing the only indication that she kept going.

The first thing he did when they got inside was to fill a bowl of water for her dog. Boomer trotted over as though they'd become best friends. Maybe they had. They had a common bond. Protecting Sadie. Nick scratched the big red dog behind the ears.

"Shower in the bathroom works. Water's warm."

"Sounds like paradise."

"This place isn't much, but it'll get us through the night."

Her gaze moved around the one-room cabin, stopping on the twin bed. "Rustic, but has everything we need. Is it yours?"

"Belongs to a buddy of mine. Keeps it for when he wants to be alone. There's nothing and no one around for miles."

"He knows we're here?"

"Doesn't need to."

"How do you know he won't come walking through that door any minute? Or, worse, in the middle of the night, and scare us to death?"

"He's out of the country right now. We met in the military. He's career." He walked to the bathroom and back, delivering a dark green towel. "He'd look me up if he was on the continent."

"Fair enough."

"This place isn't exactly the Ritz-Carlton, but it serves our purpose for tonight."

She tugged the towel from his hand. Her green eyes sparked with her smile as she studied the gold shag carpeting, a relic from the '70s. "I had no idea the government paid so well. Maybe I should consider enlisting."

"They can be generous."

She glanced from the carpet to Nick. "No one can accuse this place of being boring. That's for sure."

"And we have the added benefit of being completely off the grid."

"Right. I almost forgot. The whole part about trying to keep me tucked away and alive." Her smile faded.

Instead of taking a shower, she sat on the edge of the bed. "So what happens next?"

"You clean up. Then, I'll take a turn." He knew what she was asking. Problem was he didn't have an answer.

"I'm serious."

"You want the honest truth?"

"Yes. Of course."

"I keep you alive tonight. Tomorrow, we'll figure out the rest. Find a good place to tuck you until this mess blows over and we fit all the puzzle pieces together." He ground his back teeth; didn't like this any more than she did, as evidenced by her frown.

"We? Does this mean you're staying with me?"

"I think it's best for now. With any luck, Smith will find Grimes, arrest him again. It'll turn out to be that simple, and you'll get a new home before sunrise."

She released a heavy breath. "I don't want a new home. Just a plain old home. I feel like I've been running so long

I can hardly remember who I was before all this started." She stood and walked, pausing at the bathroom door. "I guess it's only been two years."

He could see the anguish darkening her green eyes, the frustration and loss causing her shoulders to sag. "Twenty-four months can feel like an eternity."

"I got too comfortable in Creek Bend. Started to think I might actually build a life there." She closed the door behind her.

Everyone deserved a stable home, a base. Speaking of a life, Nick had almost forgotten about his. His grandmother's birthday party was in a couple of days. He'd been so busy with work he'd forgotten. Not that his sisters would've allowed him to be late. He'd have to ask why they weren't riding him about what present he planned to bring. They generally started a month early. For reasons he couldn't explain, a very big part of him wanted to make sure Sadie spent time with a real family.

Could he take her home with him?

Being with his family definitely qualified as *special*. He just wasn't sure she was ready for the whole clan. Besides, he'd be breaking protocol.

He rubbed the scruff on his chin. No. There had to be another solution. He moved to the kitchenette and emptied his pack. He made two sandwiches and heated soup. They had a few more minutes before the sun completely disappeared. They couldn't risk using electric after dark.

Sadie walked into the kitchenette after her shower. She'd changed into the shorts and T-shirt he'd left in the bathroom. Did her long legs feel as soft and silky as they looked? She stopped so close he could smell her shampoo and notice the freckle on the inside of her thigh. He looked up and his gaze followed a water droplet rolling down her neck and then onto her shirt. Full breasts rose and fell as lust swirled through him, pulsing blood south, which couldn't be more inappropriate.

He forced his gaze away, handing her a cup of heated soup before she could see the effect she was having on him. Stray beads of water anywhere on or near Sadie's body weren't part of this assignment.

He wrapped a peanut butter sandwich in a napkin. "I made sandwiches. It's not much but should keep your stomach from growling."

She accepted the food, looking far more excited about it than he expected. "Good protein. I used to love PB&Js."

"This is just a PB. Hope it works."

She took a bite. The moan she released wasn't his business, either. But it still stirred a feeling. "I'll just grab a quick shower. I already fed your dog. He should be good until morning. Save mine for when I get out."

Boomer was already curled up on the bed.

"Will you leave me your gun?" Her voice rose and shook.

"I thought it scared you."

"It does. To death. Even so, I'd rather be prepared in case I need it."

An emotion that felt a lot like pride swelled in his chest. "Do you know how to use one?"

"I took a class. After…"

He set the weapon on the bed. "Anybody comes through that door, aim and shoot."

Chapter Four

Sadie stared at the gun. Her body trembled. Her hand
shook as she held on to her sandwich. Boomer moved to
her side. His gaze trained on her. His hackles raised. His
sixth sense on high alert.

She didn't have enough saliva to manage a good spit.
Every bite of bread and peanut butter was the equivalent
of rubbing sandpaper in her mouth. She set down her PB
sandwich and picked up her water bottle, taking a sip to
ease the dryness in her throat. She picked up her sandwich and took another bite, ignoring her racing heart.

She could do this. She could sit near the gun. She
could finish her meal.

Every instinct in her body screamed *run*.

But she'd learned long ago her body and mind couldn't
always be trusted. They'd played tricks on her since her
ordeal two years ago, making her afraid of little noises
and shadows. Since then, it didn't take much to sound off
her alert systems and kick her adrenaline into high gear.

Calming breaths generally did the trick to help her
relax.

She took a few.

Another bite of sandwich and she'd be fine.

There were times when life called for taking one minute at a time. This minute, she could handle life. She could take another bite.

Another minute passed and she managed to keep it together.

She didn't know if she should thank her judo instructor or hug her yoga coach, but right now she appreciated them both.

A few more minutes ticked by and she heard the water in the shower stop.

Nick didn't take long to towel off.

He came out of the bathroom wearing jeans low on his hips. He tucked the gun in his waistband. The sight of him shirtless sent a warm flush up her neck.

With him in the room, she didn't have to remind herself to take slow breaths anymore. He brought her nerves down by the sight of him, capable and strong.

Her tense muscles relaxed as he moved to the kitchenette and picked up his PB sandwich.

A few freckles and a raised line with deep ridges curved below his left shoulder blade. A scar?

She shivered thinking about the ones she'd collected. "I've been thinking about something. Why didn't they just wait for us at the car? They could've surprised us. Why block the road?"

He shrugged, causing his muscles to stretch and thin, his movement smooth and pantherlike. "Didn't think we should stick around long enough to find out. I stashed a backup vehicle not far from the site. There was only one way out. They must not've wanted us going anywhere in case we got past them."

Heavy pressure settled on her chest. "So, we're exactly where they want us?"

He took a bite of a sandwich, chewing as he turned. "I wouldn't say that. I doubt they figured we'd have another escape route. This cabin is too out of the way for them to know about. It's the reason we walked all day. I didn't want to be anywhere near where they'd expect us. That being said, we still have to be careful. No lights after dark."

Sadie shifted her position, stretching her sore legs. "I have proof of all the walking, too. Right here in my calves."

"Sorry. A good night's rest will help. A few stretches will do wonders, too."

Night would fall soon and everything would be black. The small space felt intimate. She pushed off the bed and walked into the kitchenette. "You did everything else. Kept us alive. The least I could do was walk to safety."

"We'll have a few more miles of hiking tomorrow. Part two of my backup plan."

"Any chance you have a horse or a four-wheeler stashed out there? I don't think my legs can take another round of Goldilocks tromping through the forest."

The corners of his lips curled. He took the last bite of sandwich. "Boomer here will keep the wolves away. Won't you, buddy?"

Boomer craned his neck and his ears perked up.

"I doubt that." She didn't see the need to explain her dog's deficiencies when it came to being badass.

"I can help with sore calves." Nick placed his hand on the small of her back, urging her to the bed before dropping down on one knee in front of her. He took her calf in his hand, rolling his thumbs along the muscles. An electric current shot up her leg.

She picked up the water bottle and squeezed, praying electricity wouldn't be conducted. The current ran hot enough to singe her fingers. His hands on her leg felt as if they belonged there.

"You know I'm going to find him, right?"

"Then what? Put him away and start the process of relocation all over?"

"Lock him away for good this time."

"And if he gets out again? What then?"

"We'll throw away the key this go-round. I know you don't trust the law. Hell, I can't blame you. But it works most of the time. And when it does, everyone is safer."

"You said this might be more complicated than you originally thought. What does that mean?"

"All we know for sure is that the case involves Grimes and your old handler. We don't know how the two are connected aside from you. Is he out for revenge? Or is it something more?"

"So you think this could be a lot bigger than Charlie and Grimes?"

"Yeah. I do. All I have to go on so far is gut instinct, a dead marshal and an escaped convict. You're the only link I have."

"Sounds like a mess. How on earth did you end up stuck with me?"

How DID NICK explain he'd practically volunteered for the case?

"Smith asked my professional opinion about your case. He needed someone he could trust. He was leaning toward pulling you. I wanted to give you a chance to stay put." Those were the basic facts. All she needed to know. Besides, he couldn't explain to her what he didn't understand. From the moment he'd picked up her file and saw her picture a warning bell had fired and his heart stirred. He hadn't heard that sound or felt that feeling since the first time he saw his high school sweetheart, Rachael.

Hadn't heard it once since her death. Nick figured

he was broken now and she'd taken that piece of him with her.

"Where do you even start looking for a man like Grimes? Someone with enough power to get to a U.S. Marshal?"

"He runs a tight operation. No one talks. We never would have convicted him without your testimony."

"At least I won't have to go through another trial. See him again, hear his voice…" Her entire body shuttered.

"No." He didn't want her to relive the experience, either. "His conviction still stands. If anything he's made appeal impossible. I'm sure his lawyers are frustrated. We'll get him and keep him locked up this time."

"You said he moves illegal stuff from South America to Canada. To do that, he must have connections in both. Maybe I'll get lucky and he'll leave the country."

He issued a grunt. "You don't trust me to catch him?"

She laughed. Her smile broke through the worry lines bracketing her mouth. "It's not you."

"Oh, we're going to have *that* conversation. It's *you* and not *me*." His attempt to lighten the mood was met with another smile.

His cell vibrated. He glanced at the screen. A text from Smith.

Deputy Jamison is missing.

Nick pinged back, asking if this was somehow connected to Sadie's case.

Smith responded that he couldn't be sure, but his contact had said he'd been spotted with one of Grimes's men several times in the past couple of weeks.

Nick could feel Sadie watching him as he absorbed the news that a supervisor in the U.S. Marshals Service might be involved in the case. Was Jamison in league with Grimes? With Charlie?

"What is it?"

"A supervisor inside the agency is being investigated." The reality staring at him from his three-by-four-inch screen startled him. Grimes's involvement with the agency could very well move up the chain. Sadie had never been more in danger.

"Whoever is doing this, I screwed with his livelihood. A man like that isn't going to forget, now is he?"

"Not likely."

"Then he'll keep coming at me until I'm dead." It wasn't a question.

"Not if I can get to him first."

"But there's more than just him involved."

He set his cell on the floor, and added pressure to the muscle in her silky calf. "When he was in jail, his business was the most vulnerable. His men were busy keeping rivals from taking over. Now, everything's changed. With him out running free, he can focus on what he wanted to get done. And, yes, his plans most likely involved leaving the country at some point. I'd almost hoped he was going to do that before because it meant he wouldn't be coming after you."

"I'm just unlucky, I guess." She clasped her hands. Subject closed.

He could see fear in her green eyes and it ate at his gut. He shouldn't want to be her comfort.

"I noticed a scar on your back. Mind if I ask how you got it?" She turned the tables.

"A stint in the army."

"Did you serve overseas?"

"One tour in Afghanistan was all it took to figure out

military life wasn't for me. I got out when my number came up. Decided to fight the bad guys at home instead."

"We're lucky to have you here."

He cracked a smile, trying to break the tension. "*You* are not lucky."

"That's the understatement of the century." She rolled her eyes and almost smiled. "In a weird way, this is kind of…nice. I'm not used to being able to talk about being in the program. It's hard to hold everything in all the time. Pretend to be someone you're not."

He nodded.

"I kind of like not having to lie to you about my background or who I am. I feel like I'm deceiving nice people all the time. Worse yet, I'm always afraid I'll slip and introduce myself by my real name. I've always been a terrible liar. I walk around feeling like a fraud."

"I can imagine."

She looked straight at him. "What happened to the witness who disappeared? Do you know?"

He hesitated for a second. "We tracked her into Canada. There wasn't much we could do when she crossed the border with her husband and kids. They had dual citizenship, so they didn't come back. Not that it would've done any good. No one can be forced to testify unless they have something to lose."

"What happened? I mean, she was obviously ready to go to trial at one point. What changed her mind?"

He looked at her deadpan. "She heard about what happened to you."

"Can't say I blame her." Sadie's eyes grew wide as she stifled a yawn. "No offense to the U.S. Marshals office."

"None taken. I get to walk away from most cases feeling good about the job I did. Then there are those rare ones like this."

"Thank you."

"For what?"

"Not calling me lucky."

He smiled warmly but didn't say anything.

"I try to be grateful no matter what. But after everything I went through it's hard sometimes," she said.

"I have a superstitious grandma who drilled that whole gratitude bit in my head. I dreamed about catching bad guys when I was little. Hell, who am I kidding? After my father disappeared, I did my level best to become one of them. Life sucked. I wasn't grateful for much of anything."

"Were you angry?"

He nodded.

"Your family help you get through it?"

He nodded again. "Not sure where I'd be without them."

"Sounds like you have a lot to be grateful for."

That much was true. "Remind me of that the next time I want to pull my hair from them driving me nuts."

She laughed and he could feel her relax in his hands. He couldn't touch her much longer without giving away the effect. He needed to think about changing the oil in his car or caulking the tub when he got home. Anything besides the way her milky-soft skin felt pressed against his thumbs and how she flared his instincts to protect her that went way beyond the badge.

"Besides, you can decide for yourself if you like them when you see them."

Chapter Five

Sadie's jaw went slack. "You're taking me to *your* house?"

"Not exactly. We're going to my grandmother's ranch. I grew up there. I've given this a lot of thought and it's the only place I can guarantee your safety."

She shook her head fiercely. "Not a good idea."

Concerned wrinkles bracketed his full lips as he stood, then sat next to her. The mattress dipped under his weight. "Why not?"

"You seem nice. It sounds like you have a terrific family. So, don't take this the wrong way, but I'm not going." She folded her arms and turned her back so he wouldn't see the tears welling in her eyes. No way would she drag sweet, innocent people into her personal hell. Whoever killed Charlie and infiltrated the U.S. Marshals Service wasn't someone to take lightly. She still had her doubts Charlie would turn on her but she couldn't ignore the evidence.

"I don't plan to give you a choice."

"I won't do it. You can't force me. I know my rights. I can walk out of the program anytime I want." She stood and then folded her arms.

"Talk to me. Tell me why this is a problem. It's my grandmother's birthday. There'll be lots of people around. You'll blend right in."

He came up behind her and brought his hand to rest on her shoulder. Her resolve almost melted under his touch.

She rounded on him, shooting daggers with her eyes. "Well, then, I'm really not going."

"Give me one good reason."

She didn't know how to be around a real family, that's why. "Because I don't want to go. I'd rather hide somewhere on my own while you do your family stuff. Maybe it's best if I strike out on my own, anyway. Especially if the Marshals Service has been compromised."

"You leave this program and you won't live an hour. I'm trying to do what's best for you."

His words nearly released the flood of tears threatening. He was right. She wasn't ready to relent. "Without including me in the decisions?"

"Of course you have a say. We can talk about options. I care about what you think, Sadie."

She rubbed her arms. Crying wouldn't change her mind. "It wouldn't be fair to put innocent people at risk because of me. That's why I don't think I should go to your family's place."

"All of my sisters and brothers work in law enforcement. You don't have to worry about them. They know how to handle themselves."

"Then I'm sure your wife has other plans for your family holiday than to hide me." Why did the word *wife* sit on her tongue so bitterly?

"I'm not married. And once you get there, you might change your mind about calling my brothers and sisters innocent." His steel voice warmed her as a wry grin settled over his dark features.

Being this close, she could see the depths of his brown eyes. The cinnamon copperlike flecks sparkled. He was attractive and fired off all her warning systems by being this close.

Her fight, flight or freeze response kicked in, escalating her pulse.

She didn't like danger. Danger caused her chest to squeeze. Danger had her waking up in the hospital in the ICU, and then on the run from everything familiar.

She focused on Boomer, who had moved to her side, and scratched him behind the ear.

Besides, she felt a little too relieved hearing the news Nick wasn't married. A man like him had to have someone waiting at home. If not a wife, then a girlfriend. Sadie needed to remind herself of that fact because when his dark gaze settled on her, places warmed that had been cold and neglected far too long. This close, he was almost too attractive. Nick was one seriously hot package. Why was she surprised by this admission?

Hadn't she been a little bit interested in him before?

An attraction now couldn't be more inappropriate. Her mind was grasping for a distraction, she reasoned, not wanting to admit Nick's true effect on her—her body.

She held up her hand, palm out. "I'm not agreeing to anything. But if I do decide to go to the ranch, what will you tell your family about me?"

"My first thought is to tell them we're a couple."

"And they'd believe you? Just like that? I thought you guys were close."

"We are. Which is why that wouldn't work. They'd see right through it. Besides, I've never lied to my family and I have no plans to start now. Momentary lapse in judgment on my part."

The suggestion of her and Nick being a couple should repulse her. The thought of most men touching her sent her straight to nausea. Not him. What had changed?

Nick.

He was strong and capable and gorgeous. She also felt as though he was the first person who had her back in a very long time. Charlie had done a good job. But she had been part of his work, his job, no more or less. With Nick, it felt personal.

But could she trust him?

There were too many sleepless nights under her belt to convince her to let her guard down. The few private judo lessons she'd taken had helped ease the nightmares. She'd even convinced herself to keep a gun in the house, although the sight still made her chest hurt and the air become thick around her. There was something about having the wrong end of one pressed to her forehead that made her heart race every time she saw a sleek metal barrel. She couldn't even watch those popular cop shows on television.

Had she gotten comfortable recently? Become sloppy?

There was a good reason. Creek Bend had started to feel like home. She had a new life and a dog for company. There were even nosy neighbors to round out her small-town experience. She'd settled into a rustic cabin near the lake that, against all evidence to the contrary when she'd first arrived, had become her safe haven. She loved her job at the bakery, even the zany hours. And some day, maybe, she'd learn to trust men again.

Nick the radiologist had rented the lake house adjacent to hers, and had made a habit of coming by the bakery in the mornings as soon as it opened and her shift ended. She could hardly fathom the muscled man sharing the cabin was the same Nick. Then again, it was his job to go unnoticed when it served him best. So, why did she feel betrayed?

She hated all the lying. Could she continue this facade

of a life? Lie to Nick's family? Deceive more people? "Can't we just be straight with them?"

"If I could tell them the truth, I would. I need to think about it first. They're law enforcement and Smith gave me strict orders not to risk exposing you."

"I already told you I'm a bad liar."

"The past couple of years have trained you better than you think. The whole time I watched you in Creek Bend, you didn't give yourself away. If I hadn't known in advance, I wouldn't have figured it out."

"My life depended on hiding my secret." She blew out a breath and then inhaled. The warmth of his body standing so close and the scent of citrus soap washed over her in a mix that was all virile and male. "Besides, I don't know if I could pull off pretending to be someone's girlfriend if I had to."

"Why not?" He seemed offended.

"I know you're here to help, but strange men still scare me."

"Maybe we should change that." He placed his hand behind her neck, leaned forward and pressed a kiss to her lips that made her body hum.

He pulled back first, leaving Sadie swirling with an emotion that felt an awful lot like need.

"We're not strangers anymore." He stretched out on the bed, clasped his hands behind his head and looked up at the ceiling. "We have all night to get to know each other better. Let the talking begin."

"What do you want to know first?" Nick had to repress the anger rising, burning a hole in his chest. He'd felt Sadie tremble when he'd touched her. His offer of comfort had had the opposite effect on her. Yet, it was something else that sizzled when they kissed.

When he'd put his hands on her calves, he'd felt her relax. He'd even felt a spark of something else. But he'd been on the floor in a less threatening position. When he sat beside her or stood next to her, he seemed to overwhelm her.

"Where'd you grow up?"

"Texas. In a small town outside Dallas on the ranch." He'd been grasping at straws when he offered to pretend she was his girlfriend. When he really thought about it, he'd never be able to convince his sisters she was his girlfriend. Not with his history. It was a desperate thought. His family would be very keen to figure out how Sadie had done what no other woman in seven years could. Make Nick fall in love again. He wouldn't bring a casual fling to the ranch.

"Did you have a lot of friends?"

"I had a lot of family. Not much time for anything else."

"Tell me about your brothers and sisters."

"You already know I have two brothers, Luke and Reed. My sisters' names are Meg and Lucy."

Sadie eased onto the edge of the bed. "And you're the oldest?"

"Correct. But that doesn't mean they listen to me." He chuckled. "I'm afraid they all have strong wills and minds of their own."

"And everyone works in law enforcement?"

"True. I guess we all felt the call to serve. Luke's FBI and Reed's Border Patrol."

"What about the girls?"

"Lucy works for the sheriff's office and Meg is a police officer in Plano. She's married to Riley and he works for the department, too."

"I take it they met through work."

He nodded. "You guessed right."

"What else should I know about you?"

"I can't think of much else." He'd always been there for his family, his mom. His other relationships were a bit more complex. After watching his mother's pain, seeing how much agony someone could go through when the one they loved walked out on them, a piece of Nick had closed off early on in life.

"What do you do when you're not working?"

"The usual guy stuff. Watch the Cowboys in football season. I like to work a good steak on the grill."

"Steak sounds like heaven about now." Her smile was the nearest thing to heaven he figured he'd get in this lifetime.

"I can't argue with that logic."

"What about school?" She turned on her side, facing him, and propped herself up on one elbow.

His eyes had adjusted to the dark and he could see her green eyes clearly. "Finished it as fast as I could and joined the military. I was the oldest, so I guess I felt the most responsibility for filling my dad's shoes. I tried to ease the financial burden for my mom best as I could. We were broke but we stuck together."

"Sounds like you made the best of a bad situation."

"We banded together. We joke around a lot, tease each other, but we're a close bunch. Mess with one of us, and you mess with us all."

She lay back and stretched out, absently running her finger along the top of the comforter. "Sounds like you gave each other a soft landing. What about the rest of your family? Did any of your brothers or sisters serve in the military?"

"Luke served before joining the FBI. War changed him. He lost his whole unit. Came back a mess. Ended up divorcing his wife. He doesn't talk about it much, but I know he hasn't gotten over it. He stopped our youngest brother from even thinking about enlisting."

"I'm so sorry. Sounds like you guys have had to over-come a lot."

"Doesn't everyone?"

She nodded solemnly. Her beautiful green eyes filled with sympathy.

His fingers itched to reach up and touch her face. To move her lips closer to his. To taste her sweetness…

He stopped himself right there.

His thoughts needed to stay clear to keep them both alive. He sighed harshly.

She had brought up an excellent point earlier. His family would see through a lie. They deserved to know the truth so they could understand the risks. He would have to be up-front with them. "On second thought, taking you home with me is riskier if I'm not honest with them."

"You mentioned your boss earlier. Didn't he tell you not to trust anyone?"

"No choice. Besides, they're law enforcement. They'll understand. Maybe even chip in their advice. The more minds we have on this, the better. Plus, they'll be able to keep you safe while I disappear to chase any leads we get on the case. The ranch is our best bet."

"Sounds like the best way to go."

Boomer faced the door and growled his low-belly growl. His hackles stood on end.

Nick jumped to his feet. He palmed his weapon and pressed his index finger to his lips.

Crouching low, he covered the distance to the door in a few strides. Anyone came in, they'd regret it. He turned and motioned for Sadie to follow.

She was already on the ground, comforting the dog.

Good. Last thing Nick needed was for the men outside to hear barking. Someone had found them. Could be Grimes's men. Now the trick would be slipping out alive. It was dusk. He'd hoped to give Sadie a chance to rest. No luck. She'd have to make do on what she'd gotten so far.

Another thought crossed his mind. They'd have to leave what little supplies he'd brought with him. He shouldered his backpack. At least there was water inside.

The door handle jiggled.

He braced himself, waiting for the bang against the door or the cheap wood to splinter. Whoever was out there wouldn't wait long.

He glanced at Sadie. She sat there, fear and desperation in her eyes. Something inside him snapped.

"C'mon," he whispered, urging her to stay low and move toward him.

The sound of footsteps on the porch made his stomach muscles tighten.

"The door's locked. Want me to break it down?" A muffled voice came through the door. There had to be at least two guys out there, maybe more.

Boomer was quiet for now, but his ears were laid back and his body stiff. A low growl rose from his belly. He'd bark any second.

Nick ducked and rolled, keeping his profile low. "We have to go. I know you're scared. I won't let anything happen to you. Stick close by me." He pressed a reassuring kiss to the top of her head. "Don't think about them. Focus on me."

Nick's reassurance unleashed a flood of butterflies in Sadie's chest, and she breathed a notch below panic.

The voice outside was familiar. "I know him."

"Is it one of Grimes's men?"

"Y-y-yes." Her throat tried to close from panic. She refused to buckle and let them freak her out.

"I'm here. Nothing's going to hurt you this time." He slipped on his T-shirt and work boots, the motion pulled taut skin over thick ridges of pure hard muscle. His movements were fluid, almost graceful, as he found his way back to her and wound their fingers together.

Boomer growled his low-belly growl again. The rapid-fire barks bubbled just below the surface.

Nick's gaze moved from her dog to her. "You think he'll keep calm?"

"As long as my hand is on his back, he knows not to bark." At least she prayed he would. It had worked in training, but this was real-world. And nothing about this situation could be simulated in training mode. Besides, he wasn't some German shepherd or pit bull ready to lock jaws on an intruder the second they showed their face. This was Boomer, her sweet dog who was meant to be her companion.

"Then keep it there." Nick slid her boots on for her.

"It's okay, boy." She hated that her hand trembled on Boomer's back. Hated how helpless she'd felt when they'd abducted her the first time.

Not again.

Not now.

Not like this.

She was stronger now.

Besides, she had two very important assets this time that she didn't have the first go round…Boomer and Nick.

He released her other hand and moved stealthily along the windows, his weapon drawn, checking each one for sounds outside.

"I'm not sure how many others there are to contend with. We know there are at least two," he whispered.

"How did they find us?"

"That's the question of the day."

These guys were good. They knew how to track the movements of a U.S. Marshal. That couldn't be a good sign.

A foreboding feeling came over Sadie, eating away at her insides.

Grimes was important, smart…but this savvy?

He was also devious, and that scared her almost as much.

She watched as a shadow moved around the room. Thankfully, her eyes had adjusted to the dark a long time ago so she could see clearly.

A blast shattered the window near the bed, sending shards of glass splintering in all directions.

Chapter Six

The plywood door blasted open, smacking against the wall. An imposing man burst through. The tall, burly figure aimed a gun at Sadie.

Boomer fired rapid barks, holding his ground in a low stance between her and the intruder.

Sadie scanned the room for Nick, didn't see him.

The crunch of glass breaking sounded from behind. She spun around. A male figure framed the window, sealing the other exit. He had streaks of blond in his long hair and the build of an athlete on steroids. There was no place to run or hide.

Boomer surged, his collar slipped through Sadie's fingers. He lunged at the man coming from behind, startling him enough to back him off. The reprieve would be short-lived and Sadie knew it.

Nick lunged from a corner. He disarmed the burly man breeching the door. Burly head-butted Nick, causing him to spit blood. A savage look narrowed Nick's dark eyes as he shoved Burly's face against the wall and twisted his arm behind his back. "I'm Marshal Campbell. And you're under arrest."

Burly twisted free at the same time a shot fired from the window area.

Sadie's heart lurched.

Had the bullet hit Boomer? Nick? Her?

Relief flooded her when she saw a red dot flowering on Burly's shoulder. The bullet meant for Nick had been a few inches wide. Boomer launched another attack toward the window. Steroids ducked.

Nick's gun lay on the floor in between her and Steroids. Could she dive for it in time before he popped up again and got off another round?

She tried to move but her limbs froze. Doubting herself for even a second gave Steroids the opportunity to fire another round. She resolved not to let that happen again. Her body had to move, fear or not.

The second bullet lodged in the bricks near Burly's head. He grunted and dropped to his knees. If Steroids had a second longer to aim, Nick would be dead. He cuffed Burly's hands behind his back.

In one swift motion, Nick dove and rolled, coming up with his gun and firing a round before Steroids could pull the trigger again. Nick's body was a shield between Sadie and the gunman. Nick took aim. Steroids disappeared under the window frame. Nick fired a warning shot and then motioned for Sadie to run.

She bolted toward the door.

Burly had managed to maneuver his hands in front of his body. He grabbed her foot before she reached outside. She twirled and kicked, but his grip was too strong to break away from by herself.

Boomer's shackles raised and he stalked toward Burly, barking wildly and focused on his target. He bit, clamping his jaws on Burly's forearm.

He grunted. "Get that mutt off me or I'll choke him."

Sadie pivoted. Burly released her boot and clasped Boomer's throat. His yelp cut through her.

Her shrill scream split the air.

She gripped the doorjamb with both hands and thrust her boot at Burly's face. The pointed tip connected with his jaw. A satisfying crunch, then blood spurted from his mouth.

Pivoting right, she stomped her foot on his face, her heel connecting with his nose. More blood spouted.

He grunted, "You bitch!"

Dismissing the nausea and pounding in her temples—the mother of all headaches raging at her heels—she stomped her foot another time.

Burly groaned and loosened his grip enough for Boomer to escape.

Sadie hopped out of reach, glancing back in time to see Nick firing his weapon. No doubt he was trying to keep Steroids from shooting again while she got away. She hesitated on the steps but Nick was already behind her, urging her toward the woods.

She made kissing noises at Boomer and he broke into a run beside her. Thank God he listened. Thank God he wasn't hurt. Thank God neither were they.

Running in boots cramped her feet and rubbed her blisters raw, but protected her legs from being cut by underbrush.

Boomer easily matched her stride, sticking beside her as Nick set a blistering pace.

They ran until her thighs burned and her lungs screamed for air.

Nick halted at the sound of crunching branches in front of them. He pressed his index fingers to his lips and scanned the woods. More broken stick noises came from behind. Rapidly. Push forward and they'd run into whoever was there. Going back wasn't an option, either.

"What do we do?" Sadie whispered.

"Follow me. We'll find a hiding spot and wait them out." Nick led them across a shallow five-foot-wide creek.

The sun had gone down, and the moon lit the evening sky filled with a thousand stars. A chilling breeze blew. There'd been no time to put on more clothing and the cold pierced through her T-shirt. Her teeth chattered.

"Wish I'd had time to bring something to keep you warm. I didn't have a chance to grab my jacket," he whispered, leading them farther east.

The memory of his smell mixed with leather assaulted her senses.

Another noise sounded ahead. More tree branches crunching under the weight of someone or something sizable. More people?

Nick stopped, listened. He looked as though he needed a minute to get his bearings. "This way."

She followed him as he zigzagged through the trees, branches slapping her in the face.

Faint voices grew louder. For all she knew they were running in circles. In the dark, it would be impossible for Nick to know which way they headed.

He stopped running and she took a moment to catch her breath.

The voices grew louder.

Nick searched around for something. But what? Where could they hide? At this rate, they might walk into a trap set by the men chasing them.

He stopped twenty feet away and waved her over.

"This ditch should hide us. Jump in," he whispered.

Boomer led the way into the four-foot-by-five-foot hole. Sadie hopped down and crouched low.

Nick disappeared, returning a moment later dragging several large tree branches. He used them to cover the opening. "This should buy us some time."

"Any chance you have matches or a lighter in that backpack to make a fire later?" Sadie gripped her cold knees, her chest heaving. She rubbed her hands together and blew on her fingers to bring the blood flow back. At this rate, she'd have frostbite before the sun came up again. Her eyes were adjusting to the blackness and she could see the outline of Nick's face.

Boomer's panting slowed as she stroked his back.

The only other sounds came from the men closing in on them and the insects surrounding them.

The sound of footsteps came closer.

The three of them stilled. Sadie kept her hand on Boomer's back to calm him.

One of the men muttered a curse. "When I find that bitch who kicked me, I'll kill her with my bare hands."

Burly? Hadn't he been shot? Must not have been enough of a wound to stop him. Should slow him down, though. Even if he found them, maybe she could out-run him?

Another man, most likely Steroids, made a shushing sound.

Their footsteps came closer.

Sadie's pulse raced. She bit her lip to keep from panicking. If Boomer so much as growled, he'd give away their position.

She squeezed her eyes shut, willing her teeth to stop chattering and him to stay quiet. Her hand didn't move from his back.

Nick's hand closed on her shoulder, radiating warmth and confidence she didn't own.

"Keep moving. They have to stop somewhere. When they do, we'll get 'em," Steroids said, disdain deepening his tone. He spit again. She presumed more blood.

A full minute of silence passed before Sadie exhaled

the breath she'd been holding. Washed-out, weepy and running through a whole host of other emotions, she leaned back against the cold hard dirt, wishing for safety, a cup of hot tea and a warm bed.

"Here. Squeeze closer. You'll lose all your heat through the ground." He scooted behind her and pulled her onto his lap.

His powerful thighs pressed to the backs of hers, sending sensual shivers rippling through her. A powerful urge to melt into him and allow his body heat to keep her from freezing surged through her.

Or was it something more she craved?

His body pressed to hers reminded her just how long it had been since she'd been with a man. Arousal flushed her cheeks. She was relieved he couldn't see her face. Her physical response couldn't be any more inappropriate under the circumstances.

His arms encircled her waist. Impulses shot through her. She pressed her back against his virile, muscular chest and all she could hear was a whoosh sound in her ears.

Boomer put his head on her leg. "You've been a good boy today," she said.

"He's special." Nick's words came out low and thick.

Sadie tried to focus on Boomer to distract herself from the sexual current rippling up her arms, her neck. On Nick's lap, she could feel his warm breath in her hair and it spread like wildfire down her back. Heat moved through her body, pooling between her thighs.

SADIE SHIFTED IN Nick's lap, her sweet bottom pressed against his crotch, and his tightly held control faltered. Why did he already have to remind himself this wasn't the time for rogue hormones?

Hell. It was as if he didn't already know that. He was a grown man, not a horny teenager who got an erection every time he was close enough to smell a girl's perfume. Sadie's hair hinted of flowers and citrus. He needed to ask Walter why he had flowery shampoo at his man retreat.

First, he needed to get a message to his buddy about the cabin.

Nick made a mental note to circle back to this subject when he had Sadie tucked away somewhere safe. He liked the idea of taking her to the ranch even more when he thought about how much reinforcement he'd have there. Between his siblings, someone could keep watch 24/7.

She shivered and he instinctively tightened his arms around her. He expected her to move away from him, but she didn't. Instead, she burrowed her back deeper against him. He didn't want to get inside his head about why that put a ridiculous smile on his face.

The last thing he wanted to think about was how two thin strips of cotton kept them from being skin-to-bare-naked-skin. At least her teeth had stopped chattering. He didn't care whether or not he was warm. He'd survive a few nights of cold. She wouldn't. Not in those cotton shorts he'd given her to sleep in.

He could see through the tops of the branches. The winds had picked up and the temperature had dropped a good ten degrees in the past fifteen minutes. The sky was blue-black. Exactly the way it looked when a cold front blew in.

They needed shelter and food. Neither of which were in his possession. Nor were the means to get any anytime soon.

Sadie shifted position, her curvy bottom grinding against him. He half expected her to push him away, but she didn't. Instead, her hands squeezed in between his. Her fingers were near frozen. He rubbed his hands over hers, warming them.

"Thank you. That's better already," she whispered.

She wouldn't thank him if she knew he mustered all the control he could to sit there with her and not slip his hands inside her shirt and caress those pert breasts the way his fingers itched to do. Needed to do? She wouldn't thank him if she knew how unholy his thoughts were about those taut hips. And she sure as hell wouldn't thank him if she knew how badly he wanted to spin her around in his lap and do things to her to remind her she was all woman and he was every bit a man.

He needed to redirect his thoughts. What other home projects needed addressing when he got back to the apartment? Wasn't there a small leak under the kitchen sink that needed attending to when he'd been called away last-minute for duty?

He was sure there were about a dozen other projects around the house that needed fixing, as well. And yet, his thoughts kept wandering back to how good Sadie felt in his arms. How he'd remember the scent of her—citrus and cleanliness—that was all hers long after this assignment was over. Didn't take a rocket scientist to see she affected him. He just hoped she wasn't offended by the growing erection he couldn't contain. She had to have felt it. Because blood pulsed south every time she moved, and so did his ability to think rationally.

He dismissed it as going too long without sex.

He'd fix that when this assignment was over. He'd have sex with the first beautiful and willing woman he could find. Hadn't there been a few? No woman from his past could erase the naked image of Sadie from his mind; the one where her legs were wrapped around his waist and he was buried inside her.

"Better now?" he practically grunted.

"Much. I can feel my fingers again."

The sweet purr in her voice had him wanting to stay exactly where he was. But he couldn't be sure they'd be alone for much longer. He couldn't risk sticking around. "We'd better head out. I slowed those two down, but there could be more."

"One of them was bleeding. He was shot in the shoulder. Won't he need to go to the hospital?"

"Depends on how deep the wound is and how prepared they are. His injury might slow him down or buy us a few hours. Unless they sent more than two men. We don't know how big the team is. Either way, they located us at the cabin, and that's bad. We're on foot and it's getting cold out. We have limited supplies. They'll expect us to camp nearby, which is why we have to keep moving. I disabled GPS on our phones for obvious reasons, so we need to keep moving until I see something familiar. If I can give our location to someone back home, they'll come pick us up."

"Okay."

She made a move to get up and it took a minute for him to send the message to his arms that he had to let go. She felt a little too right snuggled against his chest.

No woman, not since Rachael, had felt more right inside his arms.

Chapter Seven

Sadie and Nick walked for hours before his brother messaged that he was close. Headlights were a welcome sight to her after walking in the cold black night in her boots.

Nick squeezed her hand. "I'll have you in a warm bed in two hours." He cleared his throat, seeming to catch how the last part sounded. "What I mean is—"

"It's okay," she said on a half laugh. "I know you didn't intend to say it like that." Remembering his powerful thighs and chest against her body had her thinking she might not mind waking up snuggled against a strong, warm body like his. Those brown eyes with cinnamon flecks and hair blacker than night made for a package most women would consider beyond hot. Sadie wouldn't argue.

That she was crushing on her handler also reminded her how ridiculous she was being.

When was the last time she'd allowed herself to notice a man? Or relax at all. There was no laughter in her life. No humor. No friends. No sex. Okay, where'd that last bit come from?

It was true, though. There hadn't been any sex in far too long. And nothing was funny anymore. She missed the simple pleasures of feeling warm skin against her back when she slept, or laughing at an inside joke.

If she was being brutally honest, she couldn't remember the last time she really laughed at anything. She could blame her hollow existence on this whole ordeal. Was that accurate?

Sure she'd had to lie and keep people at a safe distance in the past two years. What about before then? Her boyfriend, Tom, had wanted to get engaged. Start a family. And yet she'd kept putting off the conversation. Her skin had itched and the air had become thick at the thought of making the two of them more permanent. She'd had to abandon the notion before she could really consider it.

In the past two years, she could've been almost anyone or anything she wanted. What had she chosen?

A baker.

Someone who works in the middle of the night when everyone else slept.

Did a little part of her shrink at the idea of becoming close to anyone because of the pain of rejection she still felt with her aunt?

And yet with Nick, everything was different. She didn't have to lie. She didn't have to pretend she was someone else. She didn't have to fake a relationship. He was her new handler. It was his job to keep her safe. He was proving capable of the task. So much so, that she was starting to feel more like herself than she had in months.

But was letting her guard down a good thing?

Before she could get inside her head about what that meant, a dual cab pickup truck pulled up.

Nick braided their fingers. A slow smile spread across his almost too perfect lips. "Our salvation has arrived."

The passenger's-side window rolled down, revealing an attractive man in the driver's seat. Right away she could see the two were related. The driver had the same sturdy, muscular build. He was similar in size to Nick.

He had the same nose and smile. Other than that, his hair was lighter and he had dimples when he smiled.

"This is my little brother Luke." He introduced the two, motioning toward the cab as he let go of her hand to open the door for her.

"Little?" Luke scoffed. He flashed perfectly straight, white teeth. "I'm second-youngest. And way better looking than this guy."

"Keep believing it, and maybe it'll be true someday," Nick grunted. "You're as modest as ever, I see."

"Beautiful dog," Luke said, as Nick coaxed Boomer into the backseat.

"Thanks," Sadie said. "He's been pretty brave today."

Nick pulled himself inside the warm cab after her. She was so cold she couldn't stop shivering.

"I can see my brother didn't prepare well enough for this trip. You're an icicle. What are you trying to do, freeze your witness into testifying?" He cranked up the heat and pulled a blanket from the backseat, spreading it across Sadie's lap for her. "This should help. Or you could scoot a little closer and I could put my arm around you. You know, body heat and all." Another show of perfect white teeth greeted her. Luke seemed to be greatly enjoying teasing his brother.

"She'll warm up fine without your paws on her," Nick said quickly, folding his arms.

"This is fantastic." Sadie pulled the blanket to her chin and leaned toward the vent. "Thank you."

"Where we headed?" Luke put the gearshift in Drive and handed a steaming foam cup to Sadie. "I brought hot chocolate for you."

"You've got to be kidding me. This is heaven." She gripped the drink with both hands and took a sip.

"Take us to the ranch," Nick said.

Luke cocked a dark brow, looking as though he needed a minute to rationalize the location before he spoke. "Darlin', do you want the radio on while I talk to my crazy brother?"

"No. I'm fine," she said. Besides, she wanted to see if sparks were about to fly.

"You just let me know if there's *anything* I can do for you, you hear?"

Sadie was certain she blushed. Good looks and charm must seriously run in this family. "I will."

"You didn't tell me the package I needed to pick up was this beautiful." Luke chewed on the piece of gum in his mouth.

Being so close to him, Sadie could smell the cinnamon.

Nick made a disgusted noise from his throat. "Don't you have a girlfriend somewhere?"

Luke didn't immediately speak. What flashed in his eyes? Hurt? Anger?

An expression crossed Nick's features that Sadie couldn't quite put her finger on. Was it regret? Did Nick wish he could take those words back?

She braced herself for more bantering. Instead, Luke's smile morphed to a serious expression, and he gripped the steering wheel tighter. "Nope. You're looking at a free man."

"Lucky for single women everywhere," Nick said, easing the tension.

She made a mental note to ask about that later.

"Aren't you on a case?" Nick glanced at Sadie when he said, "Luke works for the FBI."

"Coffee's for you, by the way." Luke held out a cup toward his brother.

Nick took it and held the cup to his lips for a few seconds before he took a sip. "Thanks, man."

"No problem. I'm around until after Gran's birthday. Do I need to be checking the rearview or did you ditch the son of a bitch who redecorated your face?" All the charm in his features returned full force.

"Just a couple of bumps and bruises. Nothing permanent, like a bullet hole. I think we walked far enough out of the way. No one should be able to track us."

Sadie leaned into Nick for warmth.

Luke's expression turned serious again, all cute playboy disappeared, when he asked, "What are we dealing with here exactly? I take it she's one of yours in the program."

Nick nodded. "Except she wasn't mine before. I inherited her when her handler was killed."

"And this guy being killed put her at risk?"

"She was relocated two years ago after testifying against Malcolm Grimes and assigned to a marshal by the name of Charlie."

Luke clenched his jaw muscle. "*The* Malcolm Grimes? One of the biggest crime figures in Chicago?"

"The very one."

"I read about that case, but I don't remember you being involved in that one."

"I wasn't," Nick said, taking another sip of coffee. He leaned his head back and closed his eyes for a moment. "That's good. Really good."

"Isn't that case old news?"

"It was until Grimes broke out of jail and her handler was found murdered."

"That's not good. Sounds like a mess. And an inside job. Does everyone at the U.S. Marshals Service check out?"

"Nope. This case has a stench so strong even my boss wants away from it just in case our channels of communication are dirty," Nick said. "A supervisor who was spotted with Grimes's men has now gone missing."

"Damn. Okay, so she testified and put the bad guy away. Why come after her now? They have to know the agency would be watching."

"You'd think. My predecessor relocated her after the trial twice, the last of which was to a small town where she should've been able to live out her life in peace."

"Until her man breaks out of jail and comes after her with reinforcements."

"Exactly," Nick agreed. "Possibly with her handler's help. And, worst-case, a supervisor's."

"That stinks to high heaven."

"Don't I know."

"And you think you can help her if…" Luke let his sentence die. He was silent for a minute, chewing on more than his gum. "Even so, taking her to the ranch?"

"I know what you're about to say."

"Then you know you can't break protocol. Not even to keep her safe. And you also know I mean this in the best possible way. God knows I invented doing things on my terms. But stashing her with us? Not a good idea." Luke turned to Sadie and said, "No offense."

"None taken. I agree with you," she said.

"True," Nick interjected. "Here's the thing. Everywhere I take her, these guys show up. They're barely a half step behind. The man power they have is staggering. I thought about staying on the run. And I can. But what do I do when I need to investigate a lead? Leave her exposed, alone in a hotel room? I don't have backup on this. And these guys are one step behind me out in the open like this."

"From the looks of your face, they've been catching you, too."

Nick pressed the heel of his right hand to his forehead. "It's been a problem."

"What about your boss?"

"He told me to go on Graco protocol, which basically means do whatever it takes as long as it's legal."

"I can see your problem. No one in the agency knows about the ranch."

"I've thought about every other possibility. The ranch is the only place I can keep her safe while I find Grimes. I can't leave her vulnerable in some random motel. I need backup I can trust, which means no one from my agency. I'm counting on you guys. I need everyone's help on this."

Luke didn't hesitate. "You know I have your back. I have a hot case but you have every other minute of my time."

"Chasing corporate spies again?"

"Nah. I got a serial killer on the loose in The Metroplex."

"The one in the media? Ravishing Rob?"

Luke rocked his head. "He's my guy."

"I appreciate your offer of help, little bro. I'll get back to you on that. Let's get through the next few days, and we'll see where we're at after Gran's party. You've got an important case of your own to work on."

"Nothing's too important for family. Besides, I'm a half hour outside The Metroplex on the ranch."

"Don't you mean forty minutes?"

"Not the way I drive."

The two bumped fists. Sadie's heart filled with warmth at the obvious affection these brothers had for each other. Their love came through even when they teased each other. And they were taking care of her, too. Not even

Tom did that and she'd almost married him. Heck, when she'd caught a cold that turned into pneumonia, she'd asked if he could pick up her medication from the pharmacy and bring soup. He didn't show up for hours. When he finally came through the door, she was exhausted and in tears.

He'd asked what was wrong.

She'd said she was starving and had waited for him.

He'd given her a shocked look and had said, "You know I always play poker with the boys on Thursdays."

Where her relationship with Tom lacked in spark, he made up for in dependability—and he could be depended on as long as she didn't ask him to upset his normal routine. She'd also learned that depending on others was the fastest way to get her heart broken.

Sadie didn't let herself go there about how nice it would be to have a family supporting her. At least she had Boomer.

"You know I appreciate it," Nick said.

Luke glanced at Sadie. "Sounds like a mess. But don't worry, darlin'. I'll do what this guy can't. Keep you safe."

"I'd be dead already if it weren't for him." She wasn't sure why she felt the need to defend him against his brother's teasing. Or why her heart squeezed when Nick smiled his response.

Luke cocked an eyebrow. His gaze shifted from Sadie to Nick and back. He placed his wrist on top of the steering wheel and drove.

Sadie leaned her head back.

She woke with a start, and realized she was still in the pickup.

"Sorry about the bumps. Need to fill the potholes. Gran ran out of gravel, so more's on the way," Luke said.

Nick's eyes opened, and his hand came up to his forehead. Using the heels of his hands, he pressed against his eyelids. "Means we're home."

"I must've fallen asleep." She stretched and yawned. "It's been a long night."

She couldn't see much except for shrubs lining the winding path. "I'll be okay. Just need a boost of caffeine and then we can talk through our next steps."

"Your immediate future holds a hot shower and warm bed."

And leave her out of the important stuff? No way. "You have to let me help. It's my life we're talking about here."

Nick started to protest, but she cut him off. "Look. I listened to the Marshals Service before and, with all due respect, I'm on the run again with no home and men chasing me with guns. I deserve to be included in any plans that involve me and my life. Clear?"

Nick emphatically shook his head.

Luke parked the truck and deadpanned his brother. "The lady has a point."

"Damn right," she said, grateful for the support. "And if you don't let me be part of the solution, then I'm out of here first thing in the morning. I'll figure out my own way. I can hide. I've gotten pretty good at it." She wasn't stupid enough to follow through on the threat. Her options were nil. She had no other leverage.

"Not a good idea. Promise me you won't disappear on me," Nick said. The worry in his tone almost shredded her resolve.

She had to be strong. Depend on him and she might as well roll up the tent because as soon as this assignment was over, he'd be gone. And she'd be left to pick up the pieces of her life again. Alone.

She glanced at Boomer.

Not completely alone. At least she had man's best friend as comfort. He'd shown himself to be not only a dedicated companion but a force to be taken seriously, as well. No more Scooby Doo nickname for this guy. His new moniker would be Cujo.

She folded her arms. "Fine. I'll agree to let you know when I decide to leave. And you owe me a promise, too."

"I'll include you. But you need to remember I'm the professional here. This is my job. I do this for a living and I'm trained. Not to mention I'm damn good at what I do."

"I've seen that already," she said. Then felt the need to point out, "We're alive but someone seems to anticipate our every move."

His downturned lips at the corners of his mouth told her everything she needed to know about how much she'd just insulted him. She wasn't trying to get into a fight. She wanted to be dead clear about her intention to be involved in her own future. She'd relied on the U.S. Marshals Service to keep her alive for the past two years. In that time, she'd also picked up a few survival tricks on her own. She wasn't as naive as when she'd first joined the program, wide-eyed, believing every word that came out of Charlie's and his supervisor's mouths.

Charlie.

Her heart still hurt at the thought he was killed most likely because of his involvement with her. If a criminal was powerful enough to get to a U.S. Marshal, what chance did she have? Even with Nick watching her back, there weren't any guarantees. He'd done an excellent job of keeping them safe so far, but the government wouldn't pay him to stay by her side 24/7. Surely he had other cases to work on.

Even if he was dedicated to her, how long before Grimes caught them? His men seemed to be one step behind so far, which blew her mind. Plus, life had already taught her that depending on others brought nothing but heartache.

"I understand you think my agency let you down. But from where I sit, they've also been the one thing that kept you alive."

"I won't argue that. I have a feeling if they'd sent any other deputy, I'd be dead right now and not here in this truck."

He ground his back teeth. Didn't argue.

Sadie knew she was right. "So, you won't mind if I take more of an interest in where I go and what I do next."

"What I say goes." Nick palmed the empty coffee cup. "You don't do anything to get yourself killed."

"I'll agree to consider your opinion but from now on I make decisions for myself. Whether you like it or not."

Nick crunched the cup in his hand.

She made kissing noises at Boomer and he lumbered out of the backseat. "I don't see the problem with sharing information with me."

"Can't tell you what I don't know." Was it frustration deepening his pitch?

He had a point. Admitting he had no idea where Grimes might strike next seemed to darken his bad mood. Everything was uncertain in her life. "When you do find out where he is and what he's doing, you have to promise to keep me informed. I get to know everything, including your plans for apprehending him."

"As long as you agree not to do anything stupid that could jeopardize your safety or mine," he whispered, toeing off his shoe at the doorstep.

"Why would I do that?" she snarled, angry at the accusation. She deserved to be in the loop. It wasn't like she was asking to be sworn in or anything.

"Just making sure we're clear."

"I'm not confused. Are you?"

He blew out a sharp breath. "You don't leave without telling me first. I don't make a move without informing you. Sound about right?"

"Yes. Break your promise and all bets are off."

"Got it."

Even with the lights off, she could tell she was being led into a ranch-style home.

Despite the bickering, Nick twined their fingers. He led her down a dark hallway with Boomer on her heels. Her faithful companion. He'd done well today.

When the chips were down, he'd stood his ground and growled.

Precisely what she planned to do from here on out.

Chapter Eight

By the time Sadie cracked her eyes open again, she could tell by the amount of light streaming in through the window that noon had come and gone. When was the last time she'd slept that well? Her queen-size bed, shaker-style, with a matching chest of drawers next to it made the room feel cozy.

The decor was simple. The white sheets were soft. The bed had four thick, plush pillows. A handmade quilt with alternating patterns of deep oranges and browns had warmed her through the otherwise chilly night.

Boomer lay snoring at her side. He didn't budge when she sat up.

Poor baby. He must be exhausted after all the walking they'd done in the past two days.

"You did good, buddy," she said in a low voice.

He didn't budge.

There was clothing folded on top of the five-drawer chest. She slipped out of the covers quietly, so as not to disturb her hundred-pound hero who was now growling and panting in his sleep. No doubt, he was reliving the ordeal from last night.

Sadie placed her hand on his side and soothed him until his breath evened out and he snored peacefully again. She moved to the dresser and examined the clothes. Jeans and a T-shirt suited her just fine. Her pink silk bra and panties had been washed and folded neatly in the pile. Red heat crawled up her neck at the thought of Nick handling her undergarments. Warmth flushed her thighs. Because it wasn't so awful to think of him touching her personal things…and she knew instantly she was confusing her feelings for him.

Feelings was a strong word.

She appreciated his help. He was her knight in shining armor, ripping her out of the hands of killers. Who wouldn't be wowed by that? What she experienced was gratitude. Nothing more. So why did she feel the need to remind herself of the fact?

One thing she knew for certain was that she'd been so tired last night she scarcely remembered taking a shower or changing into bedclothes. Nick had brought them in while she was showering, saying he'd borrowed them from one of his sisters. She didn't even want to think of the current running through her at the realization she was completely naked behind the shower curtain not five feet from him.

How long had it been since she'd been held by a man? Two years.

The last time she and Tom were together they'd had their usual Friday night movie at his place. He'd ordered deep-dish pizza from their favorite restaurant on the corner just as they had every week for the entire year and a half they'd been dating. If anything, Tom was consistent. Boring?

Where did that come from?

To be fair, her ex was a little too predictable, but he was also decent. There were no surprises when it came to Tom, and Sadie appreciated him for it. Wasn't knowing she could count on someone a good thing?

Why did it suddenly feel as though she'd been settling?

Her aunt had been unpredictable, and look how their relationship had ended. Sadie had felt no need to visit the woman one last time before she'd left Chicago.

The time she'd stopped by after her first semester of community college, her aunt had practically blocked the door. Sadie's excitement at having made good grades shriveled inside her at her aunt's reaction to seeing her. She'd expected a warm greeting, and chided herself for being foolish when she didn't receive one.

When she pressed to come inside so she could pick up a few of her things, her aunt had turned on the tears. She'd complained of not having space or enough money for rent before delivering a crushing blow. She'd sold all of Sadie's belongings.

Her heart broke that day.

She'd left many of her prized possessions behind until she got settled in her new place. Between work, class and study, she hadn't had time to stop by and retrieve them once the semester hit full stride.

Gone was her mother's wedding ring. Gone was the baby blanket her mother had crocheted for her when she was born. Gone was her father's revered vintage coin collection.

Everything from her parents had been sold, stripped away from her.

She'd stood in the doorway, feeling raw, exposed and orphaned all over again.

Her stomach twisted, the pain so very real. Even now.

Tom could be unyielding, but he would never have done that to her.

Did he make her pulse race the way being around Nick did? No. She and Nick ran from bullets and murderers. Of course her blood would be pumping and her adrenaline surging. And he did so much more to her on the inside. Her heart fluttered when he was close. Electricity pulsed between them. Her thighs warmed.

The comparison to Tom was apples and oranges. She loved Tom. Didn't she?

Not the same thing, a little voice told her. She ignored it. When this blew over, she would still end up alone with a new identity, a new lie. *If she survived.* Grimes seemed intent on making sure she never had to hide again. Or breathe.

She pushed aside those heavy unproductive thoughts and slipped on the jeans. They fit well enough. She cinched her waist with the belt and pulled on the T-shirt.

After dressing, she moved down the hall toward the sounds of voices, her heartbeat climbing with each step closer. There had to be at least six or seven people in the room. She followed the chatter, stopping at the door to the kitchen where a handful of people sat around the table. Her nerves stringing tighter with each forward step.

Nick stood at the kitchen sink, looking out the window.

The oldest woman, the one who had to be Gran, sat with a large pair of scissors and a stack of cloth. She met eyes with Sadie first. "C'mon on in, dear. Take a seat. Nick will get you a cup of coffee."

Nick had already begun pouring.

When attention turned toward Sadie, she wished she had the power to shrink. She knew all of two people in the Campbell family. Nick and Luke. And Luke wasn't in the room. She tentatively stepped inside, her back plastered against the door frame. Her heart pounded her chest and her breath came out in short bursts. She almost turned back and retreated to her room, offering an excuse about needing to go to the bathroom. Families were scary.

"Go ahead and sit, dear. We're a loud bunch, but we

don't bite." Gran motioned toward the chair next to hers.
She looked younger than her years. Her white hair was
in a tight bun positioned on the crown of her head. She
wore jeans with a blouse, and a turquoise necklace with
matching earrings.

Sadie eased onto the edge of the chair, wishing she
could crawl out of her skin and disappear for all the eyes
on her, staring. "Good morning. Uh, I'm sorry to sleep
so late. We got in pretty late last night."

"I'm glad you're here. Feel free to call me Gran just
like the others. And don't worry about what time you get
up around here. I bet you're starving."

"I'm on it," Nick said, handing her a cup of fresh coffee. "How'd you sleep?"

"Fine. Better than fine actually. I almost forgot who
I was."

He gave a knowing glance before diverting his gaze
to the hallway. "How's Boomer? Still asleep?"

"He didn't even budge when I got out of bed."

"I can feed him as soon as he wakes," Nick said. Then
tension lines bracketing his mouth told her he hadn't forgotten about their discussion last night.

She needed to soften the message, set things right
with him, but she already felt as out of place as celery in
cherry-flavored yogurt.

Although, looking around, everyone seemed so at ease
with each other. The vibe in the room was comforting.

Nick returned a moment later with cream. "Pass the
sugar, Meg." He turned to Sadie. "This is my sister Meg,
by the way."

"Nice to meet you."

"Pleasure. I'd stand, but…" Meg, with a cute round
face framed by cropped brown hair, leaned back from

the table far enough for Sadie to see a round pregnant belly. "I'm due soon."

Sadie's heart squeezed. Her thoughts snapped to Claire and the baby she would never see. "When?"

"Any day now." A tall, blond, attractive man with a runner's build moved beside Meg and planted a kiss on the top of her head. His affection toward his wife could melt a glacier. "How's your back today?"

Meg's cheeks turned a darker shade of red. "It's better."

"What can I get you? Another pillow?" he asked.

"Nothing. I have everything I need right here." She smiled back up at him and patted her big belly.

Sadie had to tear her gaze away. The tenderness and love between them brought a flood of tears threatening. She sniffed back her emotions and took a sip of the hot coffee as a pang of self-pity assaulted her. Had Claire gone into labor? Was her little girl swaddled in her arms? Did the sweet baby have her mother's honest blue eyes? Her father's dimples?

The tall man interrupted her moment of melancholy, introducing himself as Meg's husband, Riley.

Sadie took his outstretched hand, praying he didn't feel hers shake. She wished Nick was closer. He was the only thing familiar to her in the room. He stood at the stove over a pan of eggs.

A figure cut off Sadie's line of sight. She stared at the hand being stuck out toward her. "I'm Lucy."

"Nice to meet you." Sadie shook the hand being offered, surprised at the strength coming from someone who couldn't be more than five-foot-four-inches tall. The term "cute as a bug in a rug" had to have been invented for Lucy. She had curly brown waves that fell past her shoulders, big brown eyes and Luke's dimples.

Luke came through the back door. A six-foot-two version of the Campbell men followed. "I see you've met the clan. Except for my brother Reed." Luke motioned toward his younger brother. "Our mother will be here tomorrow."

Reed tipped his black cowboy hat and smiled. His cheeks were dimpled, too. "Ma'am."

Sadie smiled, trying not to show her nerves, and turned to Gran. "You have quite a beautiful family." Her voice hitched on the last word. Truth was, she had no idea how to interact with a family. It had only been she and her parents when she was a child but they both had worked long hours in the small trinket store they'd owned. She was lucky if she saw them for more than a half hour before bed every evening.

"We're blessed." Gran beamed.

Nick delivered a plate of food, and the earlier chatter resumed. Sadie was thankful the spotlight wasn't on her anymore. As it was a rash had crawled up her neck. A few deep breaths and she might be able to stop it from reaching her face. She focused on the food. The eggs were scrambled with chopped red pepper and onion. A couple of homemade biscuits smothered in sausage gravy steamed. This was heaven on a stick.

Sadie wasted no time devouring her meal.

Nick had taken the seat across from her. "Guess you were hungry. I have more." He made a move to stand.

"No. Don't get up. I'm fine." Sadie's cheeks heated when she realized he must've been watching her eat the whole time.

The satisfied smile curving his lips warmed her heart more than she should allow. She couldn't risk getting too comfortable. She wondered just how much everyone knew about her aside from Luke. He knew enough.

"Meg's on leave until the baby's born. She and her husband work for Plano P.D. And Lucy works in the Victim Advocate Unit for the sheriff's office."

Was he reassuring her everything would be okay? Maybe he'd misread her tension.

Luke and Reed stood at the kitchen sink, eating fresh cut watermelon.

Gran's gaze narrowed on the outline of weapons in their waistbands. "I hope I don't have to remind either of you about the 'nothing that fires is allowed in the house' rule."

Luke shot a concerned look toward Nick. After picking them up last night and hearing the threat, Luke seemed more comfortable keeping his weapon as close as possible. He seemed to be waiting for acknowledgment from Nick that it was okay to leave his gun outside.

Nick barely nodded.

"Go on. Don't make me repeat myself." Gran shooed them toward the door.

"Sorry, Gran." Luke glanced back in time to see Nick smoothing his hand down his ankle.

His slight nod said he understood. Nick was telling him where to hide his weapon.

A boulder would've felt lighter on Sadie's chest at the reminder of just how much danger she was still in. To be in a room full of law enforcement out on a country road, and still need to have weapons within reach at all times didn't say good things for her situation. Plus, being in a room full of well-intentioned strangers shot her blood pressure up. At this rate, she'd have hives before she finished her coffee.

"I should check on Boomer." She made a move to stand, but Nick held his hand up to stop her.

"I got this." He picked up her plate and set it on the counter before disappearing down the hallway.

Lucy looked at her intently. "So, how'd you get my brother to come back home?"

"Now, Lucy, that's none of our business, right?" Gran shooed her away, winking at Sadie.

Apparently, not everyone knew the real reason she was there.

Nick returned a minute later with her hundred-pound rescue trailing behind. Boomer's ears perked up as soon as he saw Sadie and he trotted over to her side, tail wagging.

"Sweet boy. Did you get some rest?" Sadie asked, grateful she had something familiar to focus on besides Nick in this room full of strangers.

Nick's hand grazed hers as they scratched Boomer's ears and her skin practically sizzled where he made contact. An electric current raced up her arm.

She stood. "He probably needs to go out." She practically ran through the opened screen door to find a place where she could think straight.

Boomer's nose immediately scanned the ground. He stopped at a tree and hiked his leg.

The screen door creaked and Nick bounded down the porch stairs holding a plate. "Don't have any kibble, but I figure he won't object to biscuits and gravy." He set the meal down on the ground.

Sadie rubbed her arms to stave off a chill even though the thermometer displayed a number in the high seventies. "Darnedest thing about living in Texas. Never know what the temperature's going to be this time of year." She turned her back to Nick and looked out on to the wide-open sky.

"Supposed to be a storm blowing in tonight. It should be plenty cold later. Remind me to give you an extra blanket."

She turned to face him, unsure of the right words to tell him she needed to go. She rubbed her arms to tamp down the goose bumps—the chill she felt from deep within encasing her heart. "Thanks. For all this. But I think we both know I don't belong here."

"Sure you do." He moved closer, took off the shirt he was wearing and wrapped it around her shoulders. Even through his undershirt, his broad, muscled chest rippled when he took in a breath. "What makes you say that?"

"I just don't. This is your family." She gripped the top of the fence, turning her face away from him, not wanting him to see how much it hurt to say those words. "And I'm grateful for everything you're doing for me. But I'd rather stay at a motel where I'd be out of the way."

"We're just normal people. There's nothing special about us."

She looked out across the landscape. The way they loved each other seemed pretty special to her. "You have a gran and sister with a baby on the way. This is a family moment and I don't feel right intruding."

"Did anyone say anything to you? Lucy? She can be quick to judge, but she means well."

"No. No one had to. I can see with my own eyes. This is a special celebration. Your gran is sweet. She deserves to have all the attention."

"You don't know Gran. Don't get me wrong, she loves for us all to be together. But she doesn't need to be the center of attention. She's content right here with all of us running in and out. If she had her way, not one of us would've moved out. We'd all still be here, tripping over each other."

Sadie glanced around at the yard that seemed as if it went on forever with the low shrubs and mesquite trees, then toward the blue skies with white puffy clouds. "I can think of worse places to be. It's beautiful here. This where you grew up?" She leaned her hip against the fence.

"Yeah."

"Where do you live now?" she asked.

Boomer loped over, sniffing around as though he tried to get his bearings. This was a far cry from his home at the lake house. Was he as lost as she felt?

"Dallas. I have an apartment in The Village. But, I'm never there. I guess it doesn't really feel like home."

"Why'd your sister say you don't come around here anymore?"

"Who? Lucy?" He paused. "Must've been her. Everyone else has been briefed." The muscle in Nick's jaw pulsed. "Sorry about that. I'll fill her in."

Why did he dodge the question? There was more to the story and her curiosity was piqued. She told herself it was because it would be nice to know one thing about him that didn't have to do with how well he did his job. "So you get to know everything about me and I don't get to return the favor. Is that it?"

"Afraid so. Besides, some subjects are out-of-bounds."

"Oh, that's great." What was the big deal? Did she hit a nerve?

"Tell me about the accountant."

"Who?" She had to search her memory for a second. "Tom?" She'd almost forgotten about him, being this close to Nick. Even so, what right did he have to ask about Tom? Indignation squared her shoulders. "He's none of your business."

"All indicators show you two should be married by now, planning for your kids' college funds."

Anger simmered. He didn't have a right to judge her life, past or present. Besides, none of those normal things were in her outlook anymore.

"Kids? Me?" She laughed out loud. It came out as a choked cough. "That's about the most ridiculous thing I've ever heard. How exactly am I supposed to have time to push around a stroller while I'm being chased by a man who won't stop until I'm dead? How selfish do you think I am?"

He stood there as though words wouldn't form. Did he regret his tone?

It didn't matter. Tears had already boiled over and spilled down her cheeks. A family had never been more out of the question for Sadie. And when could she ever stop running? What was her future going to be like? Relocate every six months? No friends? No roots? No home?

Sadie couldn't stop the sob that racked her shoulders. Or the flood of tears that followed. Before she could fight, Nick pulled her into his chest where she met steel wrapped in silk muscles. His strong arms wrapped around her and he spoke quietly into her hair. "It's going to be okay. You're going to be all right."

"You don't know that." She needed to get tight and stop feeling sorry for herself. She'd been strong so far. This was not the time to unravel.

"I'll find Grimes and anyone else trying to hurt you, and lock them up. I have help here. We don't have to do this on our own anymore."

"You already said this is your job. And I'm glad you're good at what you do. But this is my life. And it sucks. I never get to be me again. I always have to play the part of someone else. Those bastards took it all away. Everything." Tears fell freely now. Sadie had no power to stop them. It had been two long years of being strong.

Twenty-four months of lonely nights, freaking out every time a creak sounded, and a lifetime on the run to look forward to. She could never stop or slow down for fear one of Grime's gang members would be right behind her, lurking, waiting.

And Tom?

Did Nick really want to know the truth about Tom?

Did he need to hear that Tom was stable and that was about it? He provided all the things she'd been missing in her childhood? His life was about order, routine and ties that matched his suits. Where he lacked in excitement, he made up for in stability. He was the kind of guy who would stay the course, no matter what. And she'd almost agreed to marry him for it.

And yet, she now realized that with him she'd be living a different lie. Because she never felt *this* good in Tom's arms. Never wanted so desperately to feel his bare skin against hers. Never wanted any man this much. Nick was a safe haven in a storm.

A temporary shelter, a little voice said.

Nick stood there, holding Sadie, and for a split second in this mixed-up crazy world everything felt right.

He ignored the danger bells sounding off in his head. The ones that threatened to end his career. "We'll figure this out."

His cell buzzed. He fished it from his pocket. "Smith."

He answered the call and put it on speaker. "What's the word?"

"My source has been able to identify a dozen real estate holdings. There's a couple you'll be the most interested in that were bought by a dummy corporation. One of which has had a lot of activity."

"Let me guess, this company is licensed out of the Caymans," Nick practically grunted.

"You guessed it. Word has it that Jamison could've been in business with Grimes all along."

"If Jamison was involved with a known criminal, he'd have a lot to lose if someone could identify him."

"This might explain why they've come at Ms. Brooks so hard. It could be more than revenge. He might need to make her disappear to bury his involvement."

Nick focused on the floor intently as his free hand fisted. "They can't be thrilled I'm alive, either."

A sigh came across the line. "I agree, which is why it's more important than ever to keep you off the radar. I'd initially thought we were dealing with one rogue deputy. Charlie. But, this? A supervisor? To be honest, it scares the hell out of me that one of our own could be in on this."

"I agree. It also explains how they keep anticipating my moves."

"They must've narrowed down her location. It doesn't appear that they have Charlie's file, but anything's possible. And, now, I believe you're a target." His solemn tone sent a shiver down Sadie's spine.

"Explains why they seemed so eager to run me off the road before," Nick agreed. "They would have known we were watching her."

"Another thing bothers me and makes me believe what I'm hearing about Jamison could be true. They didn't seem particularly bothered that a U.S. Marshal was involved," Smith said.

"No, they didn't." Nick paused. "If he's involved, it explains how they knew where to look for us."

"It does make their job easier."

"What did you say a minute ago about those holdings?"

"I've narrowed down two locations as possibilities.

One in Houston and one in Dallas. We can't find any information on these. I can't send anyone else to check them out. Can't risk word getting to Jamison."

Nick took out a small notebook and pen from his back pocket. "I'll do it. Give me the addresses."

"1495 Oliver Street in Houston and 2626 Brenner Drive in Dallas," Smith said.

The Dallas address wasn't far. He'd look it up on Google and pinpoint the exact location. "Got it."

"Report back as soon as you know what's in there."

"Will do, Chief."

He ended the call and turned to Sadie. Big green eyes stared back at him. The hurt, loneliness and disbelief he saw there was a knife to his chest. He wanted to take it all away. Make her world safe again.

The only way to do that was to make sure Malcolm Grimes didn't hurt her again.

Protecting Sadie just became his number one priority.

Chapter Nine

Evening had fallen quickly. Now, after everyone had said their good-nights and the house was dark, everything was quiet, save for the crickets chirping outside Sadie's window in the middle of the night. The stillness reminded her of the lake house. The place had been eerie when she'd first moved from the city. There was no hustle and bustle. No horns honking. No sounds of the L train running. Everything about living in Creek Bend had felt foreign because of her Chicago upbringing.

And yet, she'd felt an almost instant connection to the place. To the people. To the slower pace.

Sadie rolled onto her left side and glanced at the alarm clock again. A whopping three minutes had passed since the last time she'd checked.

She didn't even bother to close her eyes again. Wouldn't do any good. They'd just bounce open again, anyway. The winds had kicked up and there was a storm brewing outside.

It was four in the morning. Normally she'd be leaving the house for work at this time. An ache pressed into her chest. The small bakery had become her second home. She missed everything about it. The smell of dough leavening. The first sip of coffee she took once inside the quiet shop. All the little tasks that added up to a productive day.

Working in the bakery made her feel as though she contributed something positive to the world. There was something primal and satisfying about feeding people.

And having a routine. She missed the comfort of a schedule.

The wind outside howled. A gust slammed into the window. Her gasp made Boomer stir. *It's only the wind.*

Her morning coffee ritual would have already started. Wouldn't she kill for a double shot latte with extra foam about now?

She missed the feel of dough in her hands. The weight of it. The warmth.

She always started by mixing and weighing it. Baguettes were first, and then the sourdoughs since they took the longest to ferment. As Claire neared her due date, there had been only one specialty bread on the menu. A mini cranberry panettone.

Another blast of wind rocketed and a dark shadow crossed her window. *A tree branch. It's only a tree branch.*

While dough mixed, she'd hand-laminated croissants for the day, rolled out tart shells and mixed muffins and cookies. Some breads needed to be knocked back as much as three times before being left to ferment until just right for scaling. Each loaf had to weigh an equal amount, or they wouldn't bake at the same rate.

Tap, tap, tap on the window. *Raindrops finally fell.*

The timer had become her new best friend. She'd learned that small batch bread-baking was so much about timing. Ten minutes early or twenty minutes late made a huge difference in the quality of what came out of the oven. *So much in life was about timing.*

By now, Sadie would have been preheating the ovens. Helping wake the town with handmade treats after it had been so good to her felt right. After all, there were no strangers in Creek Bend, or so they'd said. At first, she'd thought it was their way of being nosy. She soon realized, they'd meant it. Neighbors popped in to check on her and see if she needed anything. When she'd brought Boomer home, it wasn't long before baskets of treats with cards started showing up on her doorstep.

Her heart ached for the friendly faces she'd never see again.

Time to move on.

On her agenda?

A new town. A new job. A new start.

If—and it was a big if—Grimes was found and locked up, how long before he got out again? He seemed to have connections in high places. Would he ever stop looking for her? Would his men ever move on?

She doubted it.

Another boom of wind blasted against the window, causing her to jump. Could someone be out there? Lurking? Using the storm as cover?

She slid out of bed and moved to the side of the window, trying to gather enough courage to peek outside. She thought about the guns in the shed. How easy would it be for someone to locate them? Her throat suddenly felt dry, and her heart hammered her ribs. She quieted her thoughts and listened intently.

Had she heard something? No. Couldn't be. No one was awake. Her imagination was playing tricks on her. No one dangerous knew where Nick's family lived. And they were all asleep.

She peered through the window. Nothing.

The sound of a board creaking outside her door sent

her heart into her throat. Had someone slipped inside the house? Were they sneaking down the hallway? Her pulse kicked up another notch even as she knew her imagination was most likely running wild. What she needed to do was chill out.

If anyone was up, they were probably making a night run to the bathroom, she reasoned. With a pregnant woman in the house, middle-of-the-night bathroom trips weren't out of the question.

The weather had Sadie skittish, looking for things hiding in dark shadows.

She couldn't think of pregnancy without picturing Claire. Her belly had been so round the last time Sadie saw her friend. She'd wobbled when she'd walked and said her ankles were lead weights. Was Claire awake feeding her little angel? Changing her diaper? Crying over the loss of her bakery? She probably thought Sadie had died in the fire.

Oh, no.

Claire would be told Sadie was dead. Her heart squeezed thinking Claire would be mourning when she should be celebrating. Was there any way to get word to her friend?

Not without putting her in danger.

Now she really couldn't go back to bed and close her eyes because she'd picture a sad-faced Claire.

Sadie's heart ached. Dwelling on it was only making the pain worse. Claire, her baby and the bakery were all part of the past now. Time to pick up and move on. And what about Tom? What did it say that he barely crossed her mind anymore?

When she missed a man's arms around her, she thought about Nick.

Startled at the realization, Sadie eased out of bed. She needed to get to the kitchen to get a glass of water.

Questions raced through her mind. What was her next move? How long would it take before Grimes found them at the ranch?

They couldn't stay long. She wouldn't put his sweet family in danger, no matter how much he insisted. Whether Nick liked it or not, she would move on soon. She'd need to change her appearance again. Maybe she wouldn't look too bad as a blonde?

And her name.

She would need a new name. Maybe she could pick her own this time? What about Elise? Or Brittany? Or Ann?

She hadn't taken two steps into the kitchen before Luke poked his head in.

"Everything okay?" he whispered.

"You mean aside from the small heart attack I just had?"

He chuckled before glancing down the hall, and waving someone away. "Doesn't pay to walk around at night in a house full of law enforcement officers."

"I'm sorry. Who was that?"

"Reed, Riley, Lucy and, of course, Nick."

"Oh, great. Now I've gone and forced the whole house out of bed. I'm sorry. I was thirsty." She pulled a glass from the cupboard.

"No trouble. I'll let everyone know." He disappeared down the hall before she could thank him.

She poured water and took a sip, not ready to go back to bed. She hadn't meant to interrupt everyone's much-needed rest, even if relief washed over her knowing an intruder wouldn't get through those doors unnoticed.

She didn't realize she'd pulled out a mixing bowl and located a bag of flour until she looked down. A lamppost streamed light through the kitchen window. It was enough to see what she was doing. Her actions at the bakery had become so routine she could do them in the dark if she needed to. She mixed yeast into the flour, then added butter and water. When she'd beaten them thoroughly, she dumped the contents onto the counter. Pressing her palms into the mix, folding it over, kneading it, brought a sense of sanity and calm over her.

Luckily, the bedrooms were on opposite sides of the house. She could only hope to work quietly enough so as not to disturb anyone again, and least of all Boomer. If he started barking, the whole house would be up faster than she could say *quiet*.

Sadie pressed her palms into the dough, rolled and repeated until her shoulders burned.

Doing something familiar had her almost forgetting about the scary men chasing her and their ability to find her almost everywhere she went.

She turned on the oven and left the dough to set on the counter.

The feeling of eyes on her gave her a start. She turned to the doorway and caught a glimpse of a male figure filling the door frame. She knew exactly who it was. "Nick? I'm sorry if I woke you."

"You didn't. I couldn't sleep." He stood there all shirtless man and muscle, his jeans hung low on narrow hips, one arm cocked in the doorjamb and a grin on his face that made him even more handsome if that were possible. "What are you making?"

His words traveled across the room as soft as feather strokes.

"I got bored. Thought I would do something useful and bake a loaf of bread." She motioned toward the counter. "That should do it. Needs to sit for a while."

"Can't wait," he said, pulling up a stool and taking a seat. "You're used to being up all night, aren't you?"

"Yeah," she said on a sigh. She thought about how different he was now. Women had lined up in Creek Bend to talk to him. But they'd had no idea what was really underneath the ball cap and sunglasses he'd worn. He'd always stood to the side, awkward. If he hadn't been so shy she feared he would've asked her out on a date. Feared or hoped? The question had to be asked.

She'd almost convinced herself that she didn't need anyone. Her past certainly had taught her the same lesson. It would be a long time before she'd be ready to spend her Saturday nights with a stranger. And yet, didn't he awaken a tiny piece of her that she'd tried to ignore far too long?

It would be easy to lie to herself now and say she hadn't given him a second thought before. But what good would it do? Sure she'd been interested. She knew then as much as she knew now that she would never allow herself to get caught up in feelings for a man. She wasn't ready.

There'd been a time when she thought she had it all figured out. She'd been dating someone nice, decent and reliable. She and Tom were on track to walk down the aisle. He'd hinted about making the relationship more permanent. She'd made it clear she wasn't ready. Yet. Plus, she'd figured he was working up the nerve to ask her officially.

A case of mistaken identity had changed everything about her life.

She'd escaped with her life and nothing from her past. Her testimony had put Malcolm Grimes away for what was supposed to be a very long time.

Nick moved behind her and encircled her waist with his arms, covering her hands with his, entwining their fingers.

"You sure I can't help with anything else?"

She shouldn't allow him to get this close to her, but her body screamed *yes*.

Bad idea. She ducked out of his hold and moved to the sink, filling a glass with water.

"After Gran's celebration tomorrow afternoon, we'll dig deeper into the case again."

The mention of family caused the muscles in her shoulders to bunch. Her skin felt as though a thousand tiny ants were biting her. She straightened her back. "Your gran is very sweet, so don't take this the wrong way. There any chance I can sleep through the festivities?"

NICK WATCHED SADIE'S movements intently as she folded her arms and hugged them into her chest. "I can tell she likes you if that's what you're worried about. Everyone does."

"Not everyone. Did you see the way your sister Lucy looked at me earlier? What was that about?"

"She's protective." He stopped himself before he explained that they were all most likely shocked beyond hades he'd brought a woman into the house again. Even if it was for professional reasons. "Don't pay any attention to her. She doesn't mean anything."

Sadie looked ready to crawl out of her skin. "I'm sure. But I think I'd be more comfortable leaving you to your family celebration while I take a walk outside with Boomer or something."

Her cold shoulder made the room feel as if the temperature had dropped twenty degrees in the past second.

He thought about her past. How overwhelming a big family can be for anyone and especially someone who'd lost theirs. He needed to ease her into his. "We can figure out something. I didn't mean to make you uncomfortable—"

"It's fine. Don't worry about it. Really." She checked a timer and put the ball of dough on a baking sheet. She slid it into the oven, put a pan of water underneath and closed the door. Then she turned off the heat so the dough would rise faster. "What do we do next? We can't stay here forever. It probably isn't safe to stay here past tomorrow."

"I thought about that. Smith sent a text on my throwaway. He believes Grimes is still somewhere in Texas. The locations of the warehouses are perfect for moving merchandise from the Gulf all the way to Canada."

Sadie covered her mouth.

"Reports are saying he wants to stay close to the Mexican border so he can escape quickly if need be. It'd be easy for him to slip across the border and get lost if he feels the heat. Except we can't trust intelligence."

"There any other possible reason for him to be here other than me?"

"Smith isn't sure. The Dallas warehouse is leased to his company. He might be using it to move…product."

"What does that mean?"

"Guns, money, illegals. Whatever he needs to move through the country. These guys adapt their business quickly, keeping pace with what's selling."

"So we start looking for him at the warehouse?"

"I agreed to keep you informed. I didn't say you could come with me to follow a lead. I plan to leave tomorrow night after midnight." He actually planned to leave at eight o'clock, but he had no plans to share that information with her. He figured he'd find her sitting on the hood of his truck if she knew the real time.

"Fine."

"There's a dangerous word coming from a woman."

"What do you want me to say? Do you need me to beg? I will." Her green eyes were pleading. "I want to go. I want to be included. I want to be part of this 'sting' or whatever you call it."

If he wasn't so frustrated, he'd laugh. "There's no sting. I'm just going on a fishing expedition."

"You need someone to watch your back."

"True."

She folded her arms and tapped her foot. "Okay, tell me. Who else is going with you?"

Perceptive. "Luke. As you can see, I have all the backup I can handle."

"You said you're leaving at eleven, right?"

Was she testing him? He drew his brows together. "I'm pretty sure I said midnight. And I'm even more sure you heard me the first time."

"My mistake." She turned on her heel. Before she left the room, she said, "Throw the bread into a loaf pan and turn on the oven when it's ready."

SADIE'S BRAIN WAS way too active to sleep. She needed a little space to be able to think clearly and that was increasingly difficult to do with Nick around. It was all too easy to get lost when he was near. With him close, she started thinking about a future that might involve children and a husband. She knew herself better than that. Sadie would never knowingly put someone else in her situation.

She curled on her side, trying to ignore the sounds outside her bedroom window. Her imagination could go wild with every snap of a tree branch.

Closing her eyes did no good. All she saw were the

faces of her abductors. The sounds of their voices would haunt her forever.

She curled on her side and counted sheep. On the tenth round of that joy, she surrendered.

What was the use?

By six o'clock, she was ready to crawl up the walls.

She didn't want to go in the other room, but boredom got the best of her and she was getting hungry, too. The scent of her fresh loaf filled the air. Someone had finished the job for her.

After getting dressed, she followed the noise coming from the kitchen hoping she'd find Nick there so she could ask him what their next steps were. She froze when she saw Lucy sitting at the table.

In fact, no one was in the kitchen but Lucy. Well, this just got awkward.

If Sadie turned around like she wanted to, Lucy might catch her sneaking away and that would just be embarrassing. So, she didn't. Better face down the raging bull. Besides, she'd be out of there soon and Lucy would never have to set eyes on her again. Her heart squeezed. She would be long gone and into a new life—a life without Nick.

"Morning."

"Hey."

Great. Didn't seem as though Lucy wanted to talk to her any more than she wanted to talk to Lucy. "That coffee I smell?"

"Yep. Cups are in that cabinet." She pointed next to the sink.

Sadie gripped a mug and shot a weak smile. "I'll just grab a cup and get out of your way."

"No. Stay. We should talk."

Oh, glory. Sadie filled her mug and took a sip. At least she had coffee. "What's up?"

"Sit." Lucy motioned to the table.

Sadie took the seat opposite her. "Are you an officer?"

"Yeah. It's in the blood, I guess."

Could a second tick by any slower?

Lucy leaned her weight to one side and tucked her foot underneath her. "My brother's had it rough."

Should Sadie know what Lucy meant by that? She shrugged. "I'm afraid I don't know much about him."

"He didn't tell you about his past?"

"Afraid not." Sadie sipped the steaming brew, welcoming the burn on her lips. "Why would he?"

Lucy's eyes widened in surprise. "I just thought…"

Sadie leaned back in her chair, trying not to look as if she was hanging on Lucy's every word. The truth was she would like to know more about Nick. He already knew so much about her. She felt at a complete disadvantage.

"Did he at least tell you why he went into law enforcement?"

"Nope."

"Wow. I overestimated the situation, then." Lucy looked even more surprised by this revelation.

"All I know about your brother is that he works for the U.S. Marshals Service. He is my handler while I'm on the run from men who want to see me dead. But you already know that, right?" It was more statement than question.

Lucy nodded.

"So, if there's something you want to tell me, I'm all ears. But I don't like playing games." Sadie was being bold, and she knew it. But Lucy would not intimidate her, dammit.

Lucy's jaw went slack. A beat passed. She sat up stiffly and said, "I knew there was something about you I liked."

The pair burst into laughter, shattering the tension that had been between them.

Sadie spoke first. "If there's something you think I should know about Nick, tell me now."

Chapter Ten

Lucy shifted in her seat. Her expression darkened and her gaze focused out the window. Sadness overcame her once-bright features. "I can be protective of my brothers, but especially Nick. I owe him my life."

Sadie leaned forward and gripped her mug with both hands. "He said you two were especially close. I can see the bond your family has. It's sweet."

Lucy's eyes brimmed with tears, but she didn't immediately speak.

Sadie took a sip and waited. She knew what it was like to try to recall a painful experience.

"I don't normally bare my soul to strangers, but my brother told me a little bit about what happened to you. I think you of all people will understand."

Thinking about what Grimes and his men had done to her still elicited a physical response. Her heart rate increased, and she found it hard to swallow. Sadie forced herself to stay calm. "I was in the ICU for a couple of weeks after what those jerks did to me."

"It takes a strong person to survive something like that. You're really brave. I know firsthand what it takes to keep going after someone hurts you."

"That why you work at the sheriff's office as a victim's

advocate?" Sadie asked, realizing her initial assessment of Lucy had been all wrong.

Lucy nodded. "When I was young, my ex-boyfriend became obsessed with me. Didn't think much about it at first. I was dumb enough to think it was cute. That it showed how much he cared. So I didn't tell anyone right away. Let it go on way too long. Then, it got weird. For weeks he'd show up unexpectedly. We'd already broken up. Time to move on for me. He had other ideas."

"The people you care about shouldn't want to hurt you."

Lucy nodded in agreement. "Tell that to a young girl. They don't always listen." She took a sip of coffee. "It got worse. He started threatening my guy friends and stalking me."

"I can't see your brothers putting up with that."

"Which is exactly the reason I didn't tell them. They'd outright hurt him, and I thought I could handle my own problems. Figured this was my fault somehow. It was on me to finish it. I had no idea what was he was truly capable of." Tears streamed down her cheek. "Sorry. It's been years. And, yet, it still gets to me when I think about it."

Sadie patted Lucy's hand. "I can see it's still hard to talk about it. We don't have to keep going if you don't want."

"It's okay. Just especially emotional lately for some reason," Lucy said quickly. "Guess we have a lot going on in the family right now. Anyway, the experience made it hard for me to open up to anyone and especially men."

Anger burned Sadie's chest. No woman deserved to be intimated by a man, but especially not a young girl. "How old were you when this all happened?"

"Sixteen. He was my first love. I was so dumb."

"You were young," Sadie corrected.

"And stupid."

"Naive, maybe. But you're not capable of being stupid."

Lucy half smiled, kept her gaze trained out the window. "He kidnapped me. Planned to rape me and then kill me. Said he didn't want another boy touching me. That I belonged to him."

"Sounds like he was a very sick boy."

"I can't believe I didn't see it before. He was a little jealous at first. I thought it was cute. When I wanted breathing space, he got worse."

"You couldn't have known. Grown women get themselves in worse situations. I hope you don't blame yourself. You didn't ask for any of this." Sadie noticed a small scar above Lucy's eye. Did that bastard do that to her?

"I tell people the same thing all the time. Strange how hard it is to believe for yourself." She paused a beat. "My family didn't like him to begin with. I was being defiant, sneaking around dating him behind their backs. I should've listened in the first place. I could've saved myself a lot of heartache. He wasn't even my type. I guess his bad-boy image hooked me. I figured he was good underneath. Learned the hard way not every person is."

"We all do things as teenagers we regret later. No one's perfect. We learn. It's part of growing up."

Lucy shifted her gaze to Sadie, turning the tables. "I just want you to know I understand your fears. What you went through was hell. And my brother told me it was all a mistake. You weren't involved in any criminal activity. They grabbed the wrong woman."

If Lucy was trying to make Sadie feel better, she was succeeding. "Crappy things happen sometimes. We don't always get to control everything."

Lucy's ringtone sounded. She held up a finger and answered the call, lowering her voice.

Sadie tried to block out the conversation, focusing instead out the window and on the beautiful yard.

Lucy ended the call with, "I love you, too." She stuffed her phone back in her pocket, turning her attention to Sadie again. "He's the reason I finally decided to go to therapy. I don't want to lose him."

"Sounds like a good guy. You better hang on to him."

"Yeah, he is. His name is Stephen, by the way." Lucy sipped her coffee. She grinned. "I don't know where you come from, but there's no shortage of good men around here. If it weren't for Nick…"

"Don't get any crazy ideas about me and your brother. I'm his work, remember?"

Lucy held her hands up in surrender.

"Good." Why did her heart race at the mention of Nick?

Seeing the warmth and love Lucy had for her brother, for all her family, hit Sadie in a deeply emotional place. She had no doubt if one Campbell was in trouble, the rest would step up. Her heart opened a little more.

Sadie pushed aside her heavier thoughts, allowing the sun to shine through the opening in her chest. "Can I be honest with you?"

Lucy nodded.

"I didn't think you liked me at all."

"It's not you. I was thrown off when my brother brought another woman home. He hasn't since his girlfriend died."

He didn't say anything about that. "What happened?"

"It was a long time ago, but to look at the way he's still suffering you'd think it was yesterday. He doesn't talk about it."

"What happened?"

"She didn't see her twenty-second birthday."

Plus 2 FREE Mystery Gifts!

2 FREE BOOKS

ABSOLUTELY FREE · GUARANTEED

CLAIM YOUR FREE GIFTS

YES! Please send me my **2 FREE BOOKS**
and **2 FREE GIFTS**. I understand that, as explained
on the back of this card, I am under no obligation
to purchase anything!

2
FREE
Books

M-8801-0792-MG

Affix sticker here

150/350 HDL GF6M

FIRST NAME

LAST NAME

ADDRESS

APT.#

CITY

STATE/PROV.

ZIP/POSTAL CODE

Offer limited to one per household and not applicable to series that subscriber is currently receiving.
Your Privacy—The Harlequin Reader Service is committed to protecting your privacy. Our Privacy Policy is
available online at www.ReaderService.com or upon request from the Harlequin Reader Service. We make a
portion of our mailing list available to reputable third parties that offer products we believe may interest you. If you
prefer that we not exchange your name with third parties, or if you wish to clarify or modify your communication
preferences, please visit us at www.ReaderService.com/consumerchoice or write to us at Harlequin Reader
Service Preference Service, P.O. Box 9062, Buffalo, NY 14240-9062. Include your complete name and address.

HB-N14-TF-13

"Oh, no." Sadie pressed her hand to her chest to stop her heart from hurting for him.

"They hadn't actually made their relationship official…" She cast her gaze around the room and fidgeted. "He always gets a little down this time of year because of it."

Talking almost seemed irreverent. Sadie let the words hang in the air.

"She was killed by a drunk driver," Lucy said.

"I had no idea." Is that why he sounded so bitter at the mention of her fiancé? Or having a family? Sadie couldn't imagine losing the one person in the world she loved. Her heart ached for Nick. To lose his one true love. She couldn't fathom it. And yet, hadn't she lost hers? What she and Tom shared was different. Was it earth-shattering, world-ending love? No. Their relationship was more mature, she lied.

Had she been sad when she'd walked away from Tom?

Of course.

Heartbroken?

No.

This explained a lot about Nick's reactions. Was it also the reason he broke protocol to collect her things in Creek Bend? He understood loss.

Nick obviously held his emotions inside. Had he learned to do that when he was a kid, watching his mom suffer?

"I'm so sorry."

"He was a mess for a while. Got out of the military when his time was up, and eventually got his head screwed on straight again. Started dating. He's been out with lots of women since then. No one seems to measure up to her. I haven't heard about him seeing anyone in the past year. I was afraid he'd given up. Even though she died years ago, he's never been the same—"

The sounds of feet landing on the tile floor stopped Lucy midsentence. She stood and half smiled. "I'll catch up with you later."

"Morning." Nick grunted the word as he passed Lucy on his way to the coffeepot. Boomer trailed behind, wagging his tail as if he were home.

Nick's black hair was tousled and he wasn't wearing a shirt.

Sadie's heart squeezed. She stood and walked to the back door, making kissing noises at her dog as she opened it. "C'mon, Boomer. You need to go outside."

He trotted past her unceremoniously.

She followed him. Not because she had to stand over him while he did his business, but because she needed air. Her heart ached for Nick, for his tragic loss. Maybe he did understand the feeling of losing everything.

She breathed in the crisp air, inviting it into her soul.

The grass glistened, still wet from the storm. The birds chirped their morning songs. The sun, a warm glow, rose just above the trees. Everything about the ranch was perfection. How could a place she'd never been before feel so much like home?

This must be what heaven is like.

Or maybe it was the love she felt from the moment she saw the Campbells together. Even though Luke teased Nick that first night in the truck, she felt an unspoken, unbreakable bond between the brothers. She imagined they could get away with teasing each other, but let someone else try. No doubt they'd rally for one serious fight.

A little piece of her heart opened.

Being on a ranch seemed to suit Boomer, too. He ran

toward the fence and then cut a hard left a second before crashing into it.

The place wasn't extravagant. The barn needed a good coat of paint. And yet, it was a beautiful, serene place.

This would have been a great place to grow up.

Boomer returned to her side with a stick clenched in his teeth.

He dropped it at her feet. She picked it up, red paint dotting her fingers. No. Not red paint. She examined the stains closer, fanning out her fingers…blood. She released her grip on the stick, sending it tumbling to the ground.

Boomer lurched toward it.

"Leave it." The command came out harsher than she'd planned.

He froze.

She kicked the stick, launching it into the air while distracting Boomer with kissing noises.

She scanned the tree line, the barn, the fence. Her heart jackhammered her ribs with painful stabs.

Where'd the blood come from? Boomer's mouth? Maybe the stick had jabbed his gums and caused them to bleed. She bent down to get a better look in his mouth and opened his jaw flaps. "You okay, boy?"

She examined her fingers. His saliva mixed with blood. "Did you cut your gums with that stick?"

Her warning bells sounded. She stood and glanced around one more time, ignoring the chill racing up her spine. Could someone be out there? Waiting for the right moment to strike?

The explanation was right in front of her, on her hand. The sight of blood still goose bumped her flesh.

She opened the door to see Nick standing near the coffeemaker. Seeing him there had a similar effect to feeling morning sunshine on her face.

The door creaked closed behind her and she turned long enough to lock it.

"Everything okay?" Nick asked, studying her expression.

"Yeah. Fine." She didn't want to tell him every shadow made her jump. Being cautious was one thing. Letting her fear get the best of her was something totally different. She washed her hands and poured a bowl of water for Boomer before setting it on the floor. "I need to pick up dog food. Anything around here he can eat until I can get to a store?"

"I can make a trip into town later. I'll find something for him in the meantime." He turned and searched the pantry. A minute later, he poked his head out. "The bread turned out to be pretty amazing. I had to fight my brothers to save a piece for you." He pointed to the counter by the stove. "I missed waking up to that smell first thing in the morning."

A chunk had been neatly wrapped for her and placed on the kitchen island.

Sadie peeled open the Saran wrap and took a bite after pouring a fresh cup of coffee. "You finished it?"

"We make a good team." Nick stepped out of the pantry. "Nothing in there for our boy to eat."

She liked the sound of the words *our boy.*

Luke strolled in, rubbing his eyes. "I'm going in this morning for supplies. What do you need?"

"Food for Boomer," Sadie said then frowned.

"What's wrong?" Luke asked.

"I just realized that I don't have any way to pay for food or anything else. I lost my wallet along with my purse when the bakery caught fire."

"You don't need money." Nick bent down and scratched Boomer's head. "You hungry, boy? I got something around here for you." He moved to the fridge and pulled out enough meat to fill a small pan. "I'll cook up something for him. He'll like this better, anyway."

A look passed between Nick and Luke.

"What's going on?" Sadie asked.

Neither spoke.

"I deserve to know." She stood her ground.

Nick stood and folded his arms. "I don't want my brother in town buying dog food all of a sudden. We can't break with routine. Otherwise we'll alert people to our presence. I can't have anyone stopping by unexpectedly or asking too many questions."

"He's right," Luke interjected, watching Sadie as a wall of emotion descended on her with more force than a rogue wave. "I'm surprised he let you keep the dog this long."

Panic crawled through her veins and she forced back the urge to cry. "I'm not going anywhere without Boomer. He needs me."

"I understand, but you have to think of it from our perspective. He's a liability," Luke said apologetically.

"He saved our lives," she said. Her gaze flew to Nick.

He nodded agreement. "He's a good boy, don't get me wrong. It's just the other team already knows about him. He might give us away at a critical moment."

On some level, she knew he was right. Yet, the thought of being without her constant companion was almost too much to handle. "I hear what you're saying, but no. I can't do this without him. You have to let me keep him. Please."

"I didn't say you had to get rid of him, did I? I just

don't want to wave a flag in town that we're here." He patted Boomer's head.

Luke disappeared down the hall.

She couldn't pinpoint the emotion darkening Nick's features. She'd seen it before in the truck moments before he'd said he sent someone to pick up her personal things from the lake house. A shared sense of loss? A kindred spirit? A person who truly understood her dog was the only family she had left? She didn't care. He was agreeing to let her keep the one thing she loved the most. She took a step forward and wrapped her arms around his neck. "Thank you."

She could feel his heartbeat against her chest, his rapid rhythm matching hers. His arms encircled her waist. His body, flush with hers, caused sensual heat to pulse through her.

She wouldn't argue that she felt drawn to Nick from the start, even when she thought he was a nerdy radiologist. Getting to know him better was only deepening the attraction.

"Don't mention it," he said, his low baritone vibrating over her already sensitized skin.

Sadie took a step back, trying to get her bearings and erase his warm body and citrus soap scent from her thoughts. He was masculinity personified. Her mind tried to wrap around the fact the air could be charged with so much chemistry and heat in such a short time.

She suddenly remembered Luke could walk in any second. Embarrassment crawled up her neck in a rash as she glanced around.

She focused on Boomer. "He did good yesterday."

Nick cleared his throat. "Sure did. He's not the only one. He'd make a good officer, wouldn't you, boy? We'll figure out a way to keep him."

Sadie should feel relief. She was getting what she wanted. Or was she?

The past few minutes had her suddenly wanting more…she wanted the whole package. Would she ever have a house with the white picket fence and the perfect man to go along with the dog? Was Nick that perfect man?

Whoa. She was seriously getting ahead of herself.

There was an undeniable sexual current running between them. But real feelings? Wasn't it way too early to tell?

A short, well-kept curly-haired woman who looked to be in her late fifties walked in the back door. "Boys, come help me get bags from the car."

Luke didn't make eye contact with Sadie or Nick as he walked by, and out the door. He'd already said his piece about Nick breaking protocol to bring her to the ranch. Now she was practically throwing herself at him in front of his brother.

Nick introduced Sadie to his mother—she had the same thick black hair as him. Hers curled around her ears. She couldn't have been more than five foot four. Her arms were filled with grocery bags. Her wide brown eyes took Sadie in for a minute before she spoke. "You must be Sadie." His mom looked her up and down with a smile.

"Nice to meet you," Sadie said. "Let me help with those."

"The pleasure is mine, sweetheart. I'm looking forward to getting to know you better." Her gaze honed in on Nick. "I brought the supplies. Grab your other brother and help unload the truck so we can give Gran the celebration she deserves."

Nick relieved his mother of the bags she held. As soon

as her arms were free, she wrapped them around Sadie in firm hug. "It sure is nice to meet you. Call me Melba."

"It really is nice to meet you, Melba." Sadie didn't shrink at the older woman's contact. Instead, she had an unexplainable feeling of being right where she belonged. It was a temporary feeling at best. Sadie hadn't felt as though she belonged anywhere in her entire life. Even when her parents were alive, they'd never made her feel this safe.

The memory of when she was twelve flooded her. She'd had to stay after school for choir practice. She lived too far away to walk home. Her parents had had to work but promised to be there to pick her up by six o'clock.

Choir practice ended and she went outside with the other kids.

The carpool line was long.

She watched each car go past, smiling parents picking up their children.

The choir teacher gave her an annoyed look.

She'd told them her parents would be there any minute. She prayed they hadn't forgotten like they did her school play.

They were so wrapped up in their business, their own lives, Sadie wondered if they'd cared about her at all.

She never knew what to expect from them.

The choir teacher marched her inside after waiting forty minutes at the curb and told her to call her parents. He took that moment to remind her they'd had to sign a slip at the beginning of the school year saying they understood the commitment they were making.

They didn't pick up the phone.

Sadie lied, saying she suddenly remembered they'd wanted her to walk home.

The teacher reluctantly agreed, saying they were supposed to send a note if other arrangements were needed.

She'd sworn to him they'd be fine with her walking.

He let her go.

Anger and humiliation had her stalking toward home. Then she realized she'd have to walk through a dicey part of town to get there.

Fear assailed her when she heard music thumping from a boom box. Cars with missing parts were parked on front lawns.

Sofas were used as porch furniture.

Midway up the street, several men stood around the cars, downing forty-ounce cans of beer.

The anger that had brought her there turned to apprehension. When one of the men catcalled her, apprehension gave way to fear.

Her heart thumped so loudly she was certain people could hear it from a block away.

She kept her head down and crossed the street.

One of the men, the one who whistled at her, followed.

In that moment, Sadie realized what true fear was. And how someone could instill it in her in five seconds flat.

The other men goaded him on.

Sadie broke into a run.

A voice from behind her, nearing, called to someone in front of her. A man four houses down stepped onto the sidewalk. The look on his face, the grin, was still etched in her memory.

Her twelve-year-old self picked that moment to scream.

"No one can hear you," the man behind her said, his hand on her shoulder. To this day, just the thought of his touch gave her the willies.

She slapped it off.

"Someone's feisty."

The man in front of her closed in.

"This one's spunky."

Fear and anger and abandonment welled inside her. Where were her parents when she needed them?

Yes, it had been stupid to think she could walk.

Anger had her doing that when she shouldn't.

This was too much to handle.

She had no means of escape and one of the men touched her ponytail. His hands were dirty.

Sadie shivered, glancing around wildly.

She was trapped.

"You better think twice before you touch that little girl again." An unfamiliar man's voice to her left said.

She hadn't noticed the couple standing on their porch until just then.

"I push one more button on this phone, and the police'll be here before you can count to three. I doubt your parole officer would be real impressed, Sean." The woman held up a phone.

The man they addressed as Sean, the one who'd touched her, hesitated before holding his hands up in the universal sign for surrender. "No harm here. We was just having a little fun, wasn't we?"

His gaze flicked to his buddy before settling on the couple again.

The woman had handed the phone to her husband and moved to Sadie's side. The older woman's arms around Sadie marked the first time she'd felt safe. "You best keep your fun on your side of the street if you don't want to serve the rest of your time in prison."

Melba's arms around Sadie gave her that same fleeting feeling of comfort as the strangers' had. They'd asked her if her mother knew she was alone in the neighborhood and, embarrassed, she'd said no.

Sadie searched her memory for a time when she'd felt protected by her parents and came up empty.

They'd been frantic when they'd found out what had happened.

Were they a perfect family?

No.

She didn't question their love for her. Work always came first. They'd always told her the best way they could secure a future for her was to make sure she had enough food in her mouth.

Even so, she couldn't help but wonder if they'd notice if she was gone.

Nick's mom patted Sadie's back before letting go.

She gave a quick smile and then clapped her hands together once. "You boys ready to get started? I've got a new bread pudding recipe I've been dying to try out. I've been looking up recipes for the last week."

"All we need are a few good steaks for the grill," Nick said, smiling.

The warmth on his face at his mother's reaction to Sadie put a wide smile on his face.

Luke walked in the back door, bags hanging from his arms, and winked. "You better run while you can get away, Sadie. Or she'll put you to work, too."

"Sadie's quite a talented baker. She might teach us a thing or two if we let her loose in the kitchen," Nick chimed in.

Was he beaming when he said that?

Nah. Couldn't be.

Sadie had to be seeing things.

She'd seen Nick Campbell survive bullets, lead her

through underbrush and trees to safety, and outsmart dangerous men. He was most definitely not the type to beam.

Boomer, tail wagging, walked circles in front of Melba.

"And who is this baby?" Melba acknowledged, as Gran and the others filed into the kitchen.

"He's mine." Sadie smiled, despite feeling like the odd man out in the room. And yet, everyone in Nick's family had made her feel welcome in some way.

Maybe, someday, when all this was behind her and she had a normal life again, she'd live on a ranch like this one.

The image of children running outside, drinking Kool-Aid on a hot summer's day, pierced her thoughts.

What did she think about having children?

For so long, she thought she'd marry Tom, and they'd start a family two years after the wedding. He'd wanted to give them a chance to adjust to being husband and wife before they added to their family.

Part of her thought planning everything out was a good idea. Another side to her railed against the notion. She, of all people, knew how life had a way of charting its own course for people, and especially her.

In her life, if she planned an outdoor vacation, it was sure to rain.

She'd learned years ago not to fight it. Things tended to work out best for her if she found a way to relax and go with the flow.

Tom had been order and plans and spreadsheets.

Miraculously, his plans seemed to work out. The sun even knew when to cue for him if he'd planned their getaway. She had no idea how he'd managed it, but it had worked out.

He'd wanted to graduate from college before he got a job. He did.

He'd planned to work for a company that was will-ing to pay for his advanced degree so he could save for a wedding. Check.

His last year of graduate school, he expected to date the woman he planned to marry. They'd met Valentine's Day of that year.

He planned to get engaged after dating for two years. He'd already started laying hints.

The marriage part? Well, that didn't work out quite so well for him.

Sadie glanced around at people milling around the room.

She only hoped she could survive the next couple of hours surrounded by all the people Nick loved.

Chapter Eleven

The special occasion plates had been washed and put away in the china cabinet. Everyone had settled into the family room to watch a movie. The sun was beginning its descent. Nick figured he could zip out relatively quietly.

He borrowed Luke's keys and slipped out back.

Most people confused Nick for his brother at a distance, anyway. The safest way to slip out of town unnoticed was to be mistaken for Luke.

Sadie wasn't expecting him to leave until midnight, so he should be good there. She'd excused herself to go lay down after supper, no doubt her body was still on bakery time. Adjusting to being awake in the daytime would take a few weeks.

Dallas was a good forty-minute drive. What was Grimes doing with a warehouse downtown? The obvious answers? Funneling weapons. Human trafficking. Or using it to store product.

As he opened the door and then slid into the driver's seat, his internal warning bells sounded. He drew his weapon, turned around and yanked the blanket from the floorboard.

"Dammit, Sadie. What do you think you're doing?"

She didn't respond.

"You didn't answer my question," he said, immediately withdrawing his weapon and tucking it in the back of his jeans.

"Um, I guess there's no point pretending it's not me." She gave the universal sign of surrender and smiled.

She was kidding around? Trying to make light of the situation? He didn't think so.

"I don't appreciate this at all. What kind of relationship will we have if I can't trust you?" He immediately realized just how hypocritical he sounded.

She gave him a "go to Hades" look that could set ice on fire. "My thoughts exactly."

"Point taken," he conceded, offering a hand up. "How'd you know I was leaving early?"

"I wasn't sure. I guessed. Why? What does it matter? I'm here. That's the most important thing." She hopped over the seat and eased onto the passenger's side.

"No. It isn't." He deadpanned her. "You're not coming."

"Yes, I am. Please. I promise to stay in the truck." Her green eyes pleaded, and his heart stuttered.

"No, you won't." He let out a suppressed laugh. Not a good idea to let her affect his decisions. He'd crossed a line with her physically. Couldn't say he was especially sorry for holding her in the kitchen. But that's where it had to end. When it came to his investigation, there was no give-and-take. She might jeopardize his information-gathering mission.

"I will. Just let me come with you. I'll do whatever you say."

He could think of a few interesting suggestions with their bodies this close. None of them involved work. "Give me one good reason not to haul you out of this truck."

"Because I'm scared something will happen to you if

you go alone and you said Luke was coming. Because my conscious wouldn't be able to handle knowing you'd gone alone. Because maybe I can help."

She was concerned about his safety? "That's three."

"I'm scared."

In a split second, she scooted next to him. Before he could argue, her lips found his. All rational thought as to why he shouldn't allow this to happen flew out his brain when he tasted her sweet lips.

With her mouth moving against his, wasn't as if he could stop himself. He took hold of her neck and positioned her head exactly where he wanted her. Desire was a current running through him, seeking an outlet. This close, the scent of her flooded him. His body so in tune with hers, he was already getting excited. Blood pulsed thickly to the erection growing in his jeans.

He laid her back against the seat, his heft covering her. Her tongue battled with his in the best war he'd ever waged. She tasted sweet, and he wanted more. Now. Not a good idea.

With great effort, he disengaged. "You sure this is what you want?"

Her hands slipped inside his shirt, feeling their way up his chest in answer.

She tasted better than the fresh-baked-bread-and-lily scent he'd first been attracted to. He hadn't forgotten the brief kiss they'd shared at the cabin. He'd had to break apart too soon for his liking.

He cupped her full breast and groaned when her nipple beaded in his palm. A little voice in the back of his head said he shouldn't be doing this. He should take a step back. Analyze the situation. *Like that was about to happen.*

He'd wanted, no needed, to feel her milky skin against

him. It had been too long since he'd had sex, and he was already growing hard as her fingers outlined the muscles in his chest. Her hands came up to his shoulders, pressing deep.

His body ached to feel her naked and positioned right where he wanted her underneath him. Then again, he wouldn't complain if she decided to take charge and climb on top, either. She wrapped her legs around his hips, denim on denim, and he thrust his hips deeper inside the V of her legs.

His tongue slicked across her lips and he swallowed her moan.

Much more and he wouldn't be able to quit.

To hell with that. Another second and his control would be shattered.

Every bit of his body battled against his logical mind. He pulled on all the restraint he could muster to break away from her. "You make one hell of an argument, but if you don't stop this right now, I won't be able to. Your lips are the sweetest things I've ever tasted."

"Then what's stopping you?"

"I don't want you to regret anything you do with me, for one."

The sun was an orange glow in the distance.

She looked up at him, all big green eyes and full pink lips. "Then don't stop. I want you to make love to me right here. And then I want to go with you."

The first part? No problem.

The second presented the hiccup. He had no plans to take her with him. And yet, all he had to do was give her a quick nod, and he'd be in paradise in the time it took them to strip.

He had no doubt it'd be the best sex of his life.

But then what?

Their physical connection would be built on a lie. Not exactly the way he'd planned to start their relationship.

Relationship?

Whatever this was. No good could come of deceit.

She looked up at him, desire darkening those incredible green eyes. Didn't seem as though she planned to make this easy. Did she have any idea how easy it would be to rip open the condom in his wallet and show her how sexy and desirable she was right then and there? He wanted nothing more than to thrust himself deeper inside the V of her legs without all that denim getting in the way…to allow her to wrap those naked silky legs around him.

The heat had been building between them since he'd broken into the bakery to save her.

If he was being honest, there'd been sparks from the second their eyes met the month before. That spark had grown into a raging fire. He wanted her more than he wanted air.

But he couldn't let her make a mistake she'd regret. "I'm not trying to punish you by keeping you at the ranch. I'm trying to keep you safe."

"The only way you can guarantee that is to keep me with you. Besides, you've waited too long to kiss me. Is there something wrong with me? Don't you find me attractive?"

She shifted her weight underneath him, and his erection throbbed.

If she wasn't going to stop this, he should. He wanted to make love to her. Just not on the bench seat of a pickup truck. He wanted to take his time and kiss that freckle on the inside of her thigh until she moaned.

"Finding you desirable is not the problem. You sure you want to make love with me?"

She nodded.

His resolve fractured. "You just gave me an even better reason to march your butt in the house. But I guarantee we wouldn't leave anytime soon. I plan to take my time. And I need to follow up on this lead. Make sure those men can't hurt you anymore."

Her smile made him want things he shouldn't. Threatened to open old wounds, too. More alarm bells sounded, but these had to do with a totally different danger. His heart. He ignored them, dipping his head one more time to taste her sweetness.

With every bit of his strength, he pushed himself up on his arms. "So, you have to go inside."

"We have an agreement. Remember? You don't make decisions without me."

"I didn't violate—"

"No. You didn't. And I don't plan to, either. But take me back in there and I'll be gone before you get back."

He searched her eyes to see if the threat was hollow. He'd suspected it was when she'd made it earlier after they'd first arrived at the ranch. Where would she go? Just run off into the night? She had to realize she didn't have a bargaining chip in this poker game. She wasn't stupid. On the other hand, her back was against the wall. Would she be desperate enough to follow through with her threat? She was smart, sexy and stubborn.

She watched him intently as he processed the information. The minute she figured out she had him, she smiled.

He had no choice but to let her come with him. He didn't want to risk her leaving, even though somewhere inside he knew she was bluffing. Calling her on it would take away what little power she had left. He didn't have it in him to do that. He could make this work. Stash her in the truck and keep her a safe distance from the warehouse. That way, even if she did try to find him, she wouldn't be able to.

"Are you considering taking me?" Her smile melted what was left of his resolves.

"Yes."

She rewarded him with another sweet kiss that was gently pressed to his lips, which almost had him thinking bedding her right then wasn't such a bad idea.

"That kiss is to be continued later. And, sweetheart, I don't plan to be in a hurry when I peel off your clothes and kiss every inch of the silky skin on the inside of your thigh." He pressed his hand to the inside of her leg. "Or your stomach." He ran his finger along the waistband of her jeans, barely touching the sweet skin there. "Or your neck." He dipped his head and skimmed her breastbone with his lips.

She let out a sexy little moan through ragged breaths. Her jewel-toned eyes glittered with need. "I sure hope you're a man of your word."

A big piece of him cursed the timing of the drive to Dallas. He'd be a lot happier if he were back at the ranch. With her. In bed.

The thought sobered him as he took the driver's seat. He patted a spot next to him. "Buckle up."

She scooted over and leaned her head on his shoulder. "You know, if you'd asked me out on a date back in Creek Bend, I most likely would've gone."

"I couldn't. Against the rules. There were times when you looked like you could barely stand to be in the same room with me. Thought for sure I'd scared you off more than once."

"Everyone freaked me out but you. There was something about you that put me at ease. I guess it's all your training. It worked."

His gaze moved to hers and intensified. "Darlin', flirting with you was the only time I wasn't acting in Creek Bend."

He put the truck in Reverse and backed out of the lot. He maneuvered onto the highway with the all-too-real notion his feelings toward Sadie were growing. She'd put a chink in the armor surrounding his heart. This wasn't part of the plan.

What he needed to do was focus on the job ahead.

Grimes was out for revenge. They had no idea where he was but believed him to be somewhere in Texas. He'd partnered with her handler, and quite possibly given up his supervisor. Grimes wouldn't let up until he erased the woman Nick was falling for.

Hold on there.

Was he admitting she'd become so much more than a witness to him? The sexual chemistry between them could light a fresh-cut log on fire. But his heart? Not on the table.

His cell buzzed. He fished it from his pocket and handed it to Sadie, instructing her to put the call on speaker when he saw the name Smith on the screen. "You're on speaker with me and Sadie. What's the word?"

"I have good news for you, Sadie. Evidence points toward Charlie's innocence. Looks like your handler was clean. And there's a pretty good chance he hid your file before he was murdered."

A mix of relief and sadness played across her features.

"Thank you for telling me," she said.

"I figured you'd want to know that first."

Nick kept his gaze trained on the yellow stripes in front of him, leading the way to Dallas. His headlights slashed through the darkness descending around them.

This turned his theory upside down. "What else did you find out?"

"I have it on good authority Jamison is the one who set Charlie up. He threw Charlie under the bus to appease them, since Jamison wasn't having luck finding information on Sadie's whereabouts."

Nick muttered a curse.

"Worse yet, Jamison wasn't their lackey. He was their partner. My source discovered—"

"Don't tell me. Let me guess. Money in a Swiss bank account." Nick grunted the words.

"Close. Jamison had a weakness for the Cayman islands."

"So, Jamison was on the take? The greedy bastard got a good agent killed to pad his own retirement fund?"

Smith coughed. "My sources say it's worse than that. Two hours ago, a list of all Texas deputies and their personal information surfaced."

The words hit Nick like a sucker punch.

His mind snapped into focus. He knew exactly what that meant. The ranch was no longer safe. He had to get word to Luke. His brothers would know how to handle any threat. It wouldn't be safe for Sadie to return, either. He hated to think of her reaction when he told her she couldn't go back for Boomer. They couldn't go back to the ranch now.

He glanced at her. She held up the phone. Didn't say a word. He could almost hear the wheels cranking in her mind.

"Nick."

"Yeah." He was still trying to get his head around this last bit of information.

"I won't stop until I find him." His voice was nothing but steel resolve.

"Any chance Charlie stashed her folder somewhere safe?" He gripped the wheel. "Never mind that question. They wouldn't have found her."

"I'm going to send some pictures. Sadie, I need you to look at them. If you can identify him, I'll be able to get a warrant to search his house."

Sadie sucked in a breath. She must've realized the implication. "One of the guys who abducted me might be a U.S. Marshal."

There was dead silence.

"It would certainly explain why they're coming at you so hard," Smith said. "You said in your statement that you'd seen their faces."

They'd been relentless so far. It also made sense why they seemed to understand how Nick would work. How they anticipated his moves or had had someone on his heels at every turn. A man with the same training would have a better idea where to look.

Nick took the next exit. "Send the photos."

He ended the call and located an abandoned lot. He parked and flipped on the cab light.

Sadie's grip on the phone had turned her knuckles white. Her hand shook and her skin had gone pale.

Nick gently pulled the cell out of her hand and kissed the tips of her fingers. "I need to warn Luke."

His brother picked up on the first ring.

"Bad news."

A yawn came through the line. "You didn't wreck my truck, did you?"

"Nope. Much worse. We've confirmed our suspicions. This case involves some of my own."

The line went dead quiet.

"That's not good."

"My involvement in the case has most likely caused

them to target me," Nick said, his gaze on Sadie the whole time. She was afraid but brave.

"That's really not good."

"No, it isn't."

"Any chance they know about the ranch?" Luke asked.

"A list just turned up with Texas deputies' personal information on it."

Luke let out a string of curse words.

"So far, I know one supervisor was involved. He got a deputy killed to protect his healthy bank account on the islands," Nick said.

"Hard to believe someone would turn on their own for a few bucks, but to each his own, I guess."

"He's a jerk."

"One I'd like to be alone with in a room for ten minutes."

"Agreed. Problem is, because of him a good deputy was killed and many more are at risk."

Luke grunted.

"My boss is sending over pictures for Sadie to look at, so I can't stay on long. We're certain all the deputies in Texas have been identified for Grimes and his men."

"Bastard."

"Agreed. Get everyone off the ranch, just in case."

"Will do. I'll have Reed take them to Galveston. Everyone except Meg and Riley. They'll have to stick around to be close to her doctor. I'll stay at my place in Dallas. Can't get too far from The Metroplex while I'm working on my case."

"Sounds like a plan. Make Meg and Riley promise to have their place watched. Better yet, do Riley's parents live in Fort Worth?"

"I believe so."

"Any chance you can get them to agree to stay there?

I don't want to take any risks with her so close to her due date."

"I'm on it," Luke said. "I'll get the others out by tonight. Don't worry. And I'll make sure Sadie's dog is taken care of, too."

"Boomer," Sadie said in almost a whisper.

"I'll take care of him while you're on the go. You got a safe house, man?" Luke asked.

"Yeah. I'm heading to Richardson after a little trip downtown. I might need a favor while Reed's down south."

"Yeah?'

"Grimes has a real estate holding in Houston. I need someone to check it out for me. Dig around. See what they can find."

"Wish I could go myself." The telltale adrenaline that hit before a big assignment deepened Luke's tone.

"I wish we could go together. I like my odds better if I have someone I can trust backing me up."

"I'll tell Reed. Text the address."

"Will do."

"When this is over, you should come on over to our side. FBI needs more good people they can trust," Luke said, using his sense of humor to lighten the mood.

"Believe me, after this assignment, I'd almost consider it."

"If we were smart, we'd leave our day jobs and work for ourselves."

"Another tempting idea. Have Reed give me a call as soon as he gets to that warehouse."

"Can I give him a heads-up on what he might expect to find?"

"Wish I could help."

"That close to the border, Grimes might be moving product in through Galveston," Luke said.

"Yeah. I have no idea what to expect. All I know is he has a straight line up to Canada."

"You've found the right man for the job if they're hauling stuff through the Gulf," Luke agreed.

"His department might find something interesting. He'll need a reason to search the place officially."

"Reed can be damn inventive when he needs to be." Luke paused. "Keep me in the loop."

Nick agreed and ended the call. He had eight text messages waiting. He opened the first and showed the picture to Sadie.

She shook her head.

The second received the same response.

The third, fourth and fifth had the same affect.

When he opened the sixth and glanced up, he saw recognition stamped all over Sadie's features. Her pupils dilated and her breath came out in a gasp.

"That's him."

Chapter Twelve

"This guy looks familiar?" Nick asked. Anger rose inside him as he watched a tremor rock her body.

Her chin came up, and she locked gazes. "Yes."

He fired off a confirmation text to Smith.

"He was one of the guys who abducted me," she said, her body shaking. "I'd been grocery shopping. I was putting the bags in my car when all of a sudden this van pulled up behind me, blocking my car. I didn't think much about it. I mean, I lived in a relatively safe suburb. I actually thought the driver was about to ask for directions when this man came out of nowhere from behind the van. He put some kind of cloth over my mouth. I couldn't scream. I couldn't fight. I couldn't believe this was happening to me in broad daylight. The smell of whatever was in that cloth burned my nose and eyes."

Nick's fists clenched and released. He was more determined than ever to stop whoever was after the woman he was falling for. Forcing Sadie to remember such a heinous experience went against every fiber of his being. He'd buried his own bad memories so deep hell itself could rise up and not find them. Except remembering might just save her life.

Causing her more pain ate at his gut. Everything she'd been through was totally bogus.

She was in trouble. So was he. His feelings ran deeper than he should allow. He still wasn't sure what the hell to do with them. No one since Rachael had touched his heart so deeply or threatened to crack his tough veneer and he still hadn't figured out why he'd kept her ring in his pocket for a year. He figured something inside him didn't work right after watching his mom's pain and deciding love was about the cruelest thing that could happen to a person. He assumed that part of his heart had been closed off forever. "The whole scenario had to be scary as hell."

"Yeah, panic didn't cover it. I felt so helpless. Next thing I knew I woke up in the back of the van, and that guy was staring at me."

Nick didn't say the agent must've expected to kill her if he let her see his face. "You're safe now. That's the important thing."

A car pulled into the lot.

Nick checked his rearview mirror, started the engine and drove away, spewing gravel from the back tires.

He didn't want to press Sadie to talk but if she remembered something, anything, they might be able to pinpoint a location. He'd talk to her about it more when they arrived at the safe house later. Right now, he had a warehouse to investigate.

They'd been driving a good twenty minutes before either spoke again.

"Where are we going? Sadie asked.

"Brenner and Harry Hines. Near Love Field."

"How convenient to have a warehouse so close to an airport."

He exited Stemmons Freeway onto Walnut Hill and then turned right onto Shady Trail. "It's regional. But, yeah, it would be handy. If they needed to go farther, DFW's twenty minutes away depending on traffic."

He parked the truck in a small lot next to Old Letot Cemetery. The cemetery was the size of a half-decent backyard encased in a four-foot-high chain-link fence. Getting to Brenner would be an easy walk from there.

Leaving a beautiful woman like Sadie in the truck in a bad neighborhood—even locked—was riskier than taking her with him. Besides, he doubted she'd stay put, anyway. He could keep a better eye on her if she went with him.

"We'll need to keep quiet."

She seemed to catch the word *we* quickly, and perked up at the realization she was coming. "Not a problem."

"Anything happens to me and you'll need a way to protect yourself." He pulled his .38 caliber from his ankle holster.

Her hand shook as she reached for it.

"You okay?"

To her credit, she nodded and gripped the gun.

"Stick close behind me. I stop too fast, I want to feel you run into my back. Got it?"

She nodded again.

"Then, let's do this."

She scooted out his door, exiting the truck right behind him. Apparently, she had every intention of taking his request to heart. Good. He wanted her so close he could hear her breathe.

He hopped the fence and helped Sadie over. They cut across the small cemetery so he could investigate the warehouse from the back first. He crouched low behind the Dumpster in the back parking lot and watched.

There was no activity in the row of warehouses. A handful of vehicles were parked in the small lot—two vans and a couple of flatbed trucks. Everything was quiet. He didn't hear any traffic. He located the numbers 2626 on top of the metal sliding door.

They'd wait and see if there was any activity. He needed to ensure no one came or went before he and Sadie made a move to get closer.

So much of this job was about patience.

Twenty minutes passed and nothing moved except for a raccoon in the trash bin that almost made Sadie jump out of her skin. She'd kept her cool.

"Stay right here while I check out the vehicles."

Her eyes were wide, but she nodded.

Nick kept a low profile as he moved across the small lot, squat walking, just in case someone was waiting in one of the trucks. He'd learned to expect anything in these situations. Someone could be there asleep. At least he was sure no one was getting lucky in the backseat. He hadn't seen the telltale fog of the windows. Near Harry Hines, anything was possible. In his years with the agency, he'd pretty much seen it all.

He touched the hood of each vehicle. Cold.

None of them had been driven lately.

One by one, he checked the cabs.

Clear.

Good.

He returned to Sadie. "Ready to move to the front?"

She nodded again. She was either scared to the point of being mute or a good listener. He hoped for the second. He could work with that.

"Let's move."

He was almost surprised when she followed him. Meant she was coherent. Another good sign.

The strip of warehouses was encased by wrought-iron fences out front. He hoped none of them were hot. He could scale the six-foot barrier easily with one hand on the top rail, but Sadie wouldn't be able to. He picked up a rock and tossed it at the fence.

No telltale crackle of electricity.

The sounds of tires turning on pavement caught his attention. Two dots appeared down the street. The headlights were moving toward them.

He grabbed Sadie by the hand and climbed over the fence. She dropped to her hands and knees and crawled behind him.

The headlights moved closer.

Adrenaline thumped through his veins. He couldn't guarantee Sadie's safety. Didn't especially like the feeling gripping him that he'd compromised her security by bringing her along.

Wouldn't do any good to second-guess himself.

She was there.

He was there.

He'd make sure they both made it out alive.

Brakes squeaked the car to a stop two buildings down. Nick made out an older model Lincoln. There was a driver and a passenger. The passenger moved over to the driver's side and the seat flew back. Both of them disappeared.

Nick watched carefully for the overhead light to come on in case someone was exiting the vehicle. An experienced criminal would know to turn it off before slipping out. Neither Grimes nor the U.S. Marshals searching for them were amateurs.

Nick waited another five minutes, his gaze intent on the dark sedan.

"I'm moving closer to check it out. You stay right here," he whispered when enough time had passed. He had to crawl across the empty parking lot to get close enough to see what was going on. No one had left the vehicle as far as he could tell.

A light came on in the third building as he neared the halfway mark across the lot. The warehouse was right next to him. He froze, making himself as small as possible.

Nothing but stillness surrounded him.

He inched closer to the Lincoln. Made it to the corner where his lot and the one for building number two met. The car wasn't a hundred yards away. He was close enough to see the windows fogging up and hear the shocks creaking. Lovers? Not likely. Not at this time of night on this road. But they were having sex.

Nick had a problem on his hands. He could flash his badge and get rid of the prostitute and John, but possibly call attention to himself and Sadie. Or he could wait it out. His back already hurt like hell.

The light flipped off on building number three.

He had to assume whoever was there had gotten what they came for. They must've used the back entrance, which made the most sense if they were loading supplies. He didn't have time to care why a person would be here at this late hour.

Even though he knew exactly what was going on in the car, he had to make sure. Getting close enough to get a visual would be right up there with his least favorite task of the night.

On closer assessment, the pair was doing exactly what he suspected.

Nick crawled across the lot. Relief flooded him that Sadie was exactly where he left her. Not having his eyes on her for even a second did all kinds of crazy things to his insides, to his heart. This didn't seem like an appropriate time to get inside his head about what that meant.

She leaned so close he could feel her breath on him. "What could they possibly be doing over there? I freaked when they pulled up, thinking the worst, but no one's getting out of the car."

He couldn't wipe the ridiculous grin off his face. This wasn't the time to be charmed by her innocence. "You don't want to know."

"What does that… Oh." With the dim glow of a street lamp, he could see her cheeks flush with embarrassment. "What do we do now?"

"Wait."

Fifteen minutes passed before the passenger's door opened and a tall skinny girl crawled out.

Sadie reached out to Nick, placing her hand in his. Hers seemed small by comparison. And soft.

He squeezed her fingers for reassurance. A few more minutes and they'd get what they came for.

The door slammed shut and the Lincoln pulled away, squealing its tires.

Skinny tucked something, presumably cash, in her bra and stumbled away, either drunk or high, or both.

Nick didn't like the idea of her or anyone else being around or the possibility they could be seen. Her presence also most likely meant there were others like her wandering around, searching for their next twenty dollars or fix.

His warning system flared up that anyone else could see them or identify them at the scene. Especially since he had no idea what this warehouse was being used for.

He had to prepare himself for any possibility.

Damn that anyone could signal inside or send up a red flag, alerting Grimes's men to their presence if anyone was there.

"Stick close by me."

Sadie nodded.

He had to make sure Skinny was far enough away, and there was no pimp nearby working this end of the street.

Nick kept to the shadows, with Sadie right behind him every step of the way.

He followed Skinny back to Harry Hines, where she met up with a few similarly dressed women.

Relief flooded him as he backtracked the couple of blocks to the warehouse.

Instinct told him they needed to get the information they came for and get the hell out of there.

Chapter Thirteen

As expected, the front and back doors were locked. Sadie hadn't expected a man like Grimes to leave his inventory, or whatever he kept in there, unprotected.

"We can't break one of the windows up front, can we?" she asked.

"I don't want to raise suspicion we were here." Nick moved to the dock door, bent down and examined the lock. He fished a small Swiss army knife out of his pocket and went to work with his flashlight and small pick-looking tool. "I can manage this one easily enough."

"Can you do this?" Sadie asked, shocked. Surely he wasn't planning on breaking and entering. Wasn't that a felony offense? He'd lose his job. Possibly even go to jail.

He deadpanned her. "Not legally. Anything we find won't be admissible in court. But they've involved my family. I'll do what's necessary to protect them."

The way he clenched his jaw left no doubt he meant every word.

She tamped down the emotion tugging at her heart. The air stirred around them. With the way he watched over the people he loved, Nick would make an amazing father someday. He was exactly the kind of man she'd want to father her children someday.

The shock of her realization she wanted kids was only dwarfed by the one that said she wanted to be with Nick.

"What do you think we'll find in there?" she asked.

"Could be anything from guns to illegals. It's dark and quiet inside. Whoever takes care of the shipments has gone home."

Images of poor, hungry people packed inside trucks without air-conditioning popped into Sadie's mind. Since she'd been in Texas, she hadn't gone a month without seeing something in the news about human trafficker raids or inhumane conditions.

A snick sounded, and she knew he'd cracked the lock. He closed the tool and stuffed it in his pocket.

He rolled up the door enough for them to squat down and slip inside. "I'll go first and make sure it's clear."

"Okay."

A few seconds later, he told her it was fine.

She ducked down and crawled into the opening.

Nick pulled the metal door closed, drew his weapon and picked up the flashlight he'd set down.

The thin beam skimmed the large room, exposing a line of twin mattresses on the floor spanning two walls. Some had pillows and blankets, others had nothing but a towel on them. Looked as if they could pack fifty illegals in there at one time. The place smelled like sweat and fear.

Other than that, the place was empty save for shipping evidence like boxes, tape and a small forklift.

Every indicator pointed toward this place being used for moving illegals through the country, and God only knew what else. "Can you call the police? Have them arrested? It's obvious criminal activity is going on in here."

"Not without proof."

"What about those beds?" She pointed before she remembered he couldn't see her in the dark.

"Circumstantial. Plus, I can't use evidence gathered without a proper search warrant."

Seriously? "Isn't it obvious what they're doing?"

"Yes. But courts, judges and juries want indisputable evidence and an appropriate paper trail before they send people to jail. A good lawyer would shred this case to pieces."

"Seems like a pretty screwed-up system if you ask me."

"From where I stand right now, I wouldn't argue. But that's the structure. It isn't perfect, but it does keep innocent people out of prison."

"It shouldn't be so hard to get guilty people off the streets."

"Agreed." Nick ran the stream of light up a stairwell to what looked like a second-story office.

Hope bubbled. "Maybe there will be something in there we can use."

She followed him up the narrow steps.

The wood door was locked. She had no doubts that Nick could pop the door open with one good bump of his shoulder, but he wouldn't.

Instead, he pulled out his tool and jimmied the lock.

This one took even less time to crack.

The flashlight beam skimmed over the room. There was a solid mahogany desk with a leather executive chair tucked into it.

Nick moved to it. The top was clean. He tried to open the drawers of the desk. They didn't budge.

"Whatever they're doing must pay well," Sadie said, taking in the expensive-looking leather sofa against one wall, and the opulent chairs positioned across from the desk.

"Tells me something else. The big boss works from here."

"How do you know that?"

"They wouldn't approve spending this much money on furniture for a captain. And Dallas is a great place to locate his headquarters. We have the worst jury pulls. Even if we gather enough evidence to arrest them, it's harder to get a conviction here. Criminals know it. Grimes knows it. Everyone in the agency would, too."

"Grimes. Here?" She glanced around. A band of tension tightened around Sadie's chest.

"Yes." Nick moved to a filing cabinet positioned against the wall behind the desk. "Might find something useful in here."

He opened drawer after drawer while Sadie helped flip through folders.

She pulled one out. "What is this?"

Nick focused the beam on the piece of paper she held. "An invoice for silk scarves."

Sadie hauled out another one and held it under the light. "And this is for Chinese footwear."

The rest of the contents of the drawer yielded similar results.

Her heart stopped at the sound of a car pulling into the front parking lot. "What do we do now?"

Nick turned off the flashlight and held her hand. "We wait."

She had to remind herself to breath.

Was this another paid late-night tryst with the prostitute they'd seen earlier or one of her friends? Sadie couldn't allow herself to consider anything worse. Like

Grimes returning. If he found her this time, would she and Nick be dead?

Minutes ticked by.

A siren blast followed by squad car lights split the darkness.

Sadie thought she could hear her heart pounding in her chest as they waited for the cop to pull away.

Five minutes later, everything was dark out front.

Nick flicked on the flashlight.

Sadie held up another useless invoice. This one was for bracelets. "We aren't going to find anything, are we?"

"Don't give up yet." He pulled the file cabinet away from the wall.

"What are you doing?"

"I learned this trick a long time ago." He felt along the back of the wood then produced a manila folder. "Taped to the back."

"Oh, my gosh." He'd found something.

They moved to the desk. Nick opened the envelope. He dumped the contents out. There were a few documents, pictures and, holy cow, Sadie's personal information. They had the name of the bakery where she worked, which she already knew they'd discovered, and a picture of her lake house.

She gasped at the picture of her and Nick in the truck, escaping from the bakery. Whoever took it must've been with the person who'd followed them.

Her pulse quickened with every new picture. Luke. Reed. Meg. Riley. Lucy. One by one, each of Nick's family members appeared.

Nick fanned out the photos from the deck and grunted a foul word.

She'd been thinking the exact same one.

The message was clear. No way did they plan to leave his family alone.

NICK SPLAYED THE pictures and documents from the envelope across the desk after making the call to his safe house contact. He pulled out his camera and took photos then texted the new information to Luke. "I'll forward this to Smith once we get to the safe house. We can examine these more closely there, as well."

Nick figured it would be easy to hide Sadie in Richardson's Chinatown among the strip malls.

He pulled onto Greenville Avenue, located Dim Sum, the restaurant, and parked in the dark behind it. Paul Huang's new Japanese import was parked under the street lamp.

Nick flashed his headlights and Paul zipped past him and out of the lot, slowing down enough for Nick to follow. His contact was about as far away from the U.S. Marshals Service as he could be. No one knew about Paul.

A cold front was due, and Nick would at least give Sadie a solid roof over her head tonight.

Winding into a neighborhood behind the shopping mall, Paul pulled in front of a house and jumped out of his car, motioning Nick to park on the pad in front of the house.

"My man, Nick," the Asian said, twin plumes of smoke rising from his nostrils.

They shook hands and bumped shoulders in a man greeting.

"It's been a long time. How's your mom?" Nick asked.

"Ah, you know her. She slaves away in the kitchen. I finally have enough money to give her a decent retirement. I don't need the help. She can relax. What does she do? Work. She's so stubborn."

"Probably wants to feel useful," Nick offered.

"That's true. She worries about getting too old."

"You have any more trouble at the restaurant?" Nick had intervened on several occasions on Paul's behalf when gangs tried to move in on his block and force him to pay protection fees or risk having his livelihood burned to the ground.

"No. Thanks to you. They didn't come back." Paul stood staring at Sadie, waiting for an introduction.

Nick shook his head. "Better if you don't know anything on this one."

Paul, a middle-aged Asian with white hair dotting his temples, nodded his understanding. He popped the butt of his cigarette in his mouth and puffed on it while he stuck the key in the lock. He opened the door. "It's not a big place but it's clean. You hungry?"

"Nah. We're okay for the night."

"You need anything, you take it. I stocked the fridge as soon as you called." He tossed a key onto the counter next to the one he'd used to open the door a moment ago. "The restaurant is behind you. This yard backs up to it. Hop the wall and you're there. If you don't find what you need here, go there."

"I appreciate you letting us use your relatives' place for a few days. We won't be here too long."

"Nothing's too much to ask from you, my friend. You saved my life. My aunt and uncle are out of the country, anyway. Went back to China. I don't know why. I told them there's nothing back there I forgot." He laughed at his own joke and shook his head. "They don't need to use this place right now. It's no trouble at all. I put fresh sheets on the bed for you." His gaze moved from Nick to

Sadie. "If not for this guy, I'd have nothing. Those thugs almost ran me out of business. Out of town. But this guy. He stopped them." He gave Nick a friendly tap on the shoulder. "You didn't let them push around the little guy."

Nick smiled. "Glad to help."

"He's a good guy," Paul said, winking at Sadie. "He'll take care of you."

SADIE STOOD BY the door as Nick thanked Paul again.

The place was tight, but had everything they needed. From the front door, she could see the living and dining rooms, as well as the kitchen. There was a flat-screen TV on one wall and a hunter-green recliner sofa positioned in front. Pictures of family covered most of the white space on the walls.

She excused herself to the bathroom and starting filling the tub while she undressed. A warm bath sounded like heaven. Besides, she needed a minute to process what they'd brought from the warehouse.

A soft knock at the door startled her.

"Come in. I'm covered." She sat on the side of the tub with a bath towel wrapped around her.

The door barely opened, and she could see a sliver of Nick's face. "I don't want to bother you. Just wanted to give you an update. Smith has the information."

"It's fine. I was just sitting here thinking. If there's a U.S. Marshal involved, then no one's safe, are they?"

"You are. I am. My family is on their way to Galveston right now. No one knows about our place there. They sure as hell won't get to us here." He opened the door a little more and leaned against the jamb. "I just spoke to Reed, by the way. Boomer's doing fine. It's probably best for him to be with them right now."

She nodded, ignoring the ache in her chest. "I do realize that. I wouldn't want to do anything that would put his life at risk. And especially not just so I can have him with me. He has to come first."

"He's lucky to have you."

"He's in good hands with your family."

"Gran might fight you for him later." He smiled, and it brightened his whole face. He held out two beers. The label read Tsingtao. "I found these in the fridge. They're actually pretty good. Best of all, they're cold. Want one?"

"Do I? Yes. I would very much like a cold drink."

He opened the bottle of beer and handed it to her.

"Don't worry. We'll figure this out. We're getting closer to uncovering the truth. Knowing who's involved is a huge plus for our side. Now we have to gather enough evidence to put the jerk away."

His words provided a small measure of comfort. There was something about his presence that calmed her rattled nerves. He was just this amazingly calming man. She could get used to this, to him.

"I'll be in the other room if you need anything else. I promise not to peek, but do you mind if I leave this cracked?"

"Not at all. In fact, I'd feel better knowing you could hear me."

He disappeared and she set her beer down, slipped off the towel and eased into the warm water. The tension from a long day evaporated, similar to boiling water turning into steam.

She picked up her drink. Beads of water dripped down the longneck bottle as she curled her fingers around the base. The light taste and cool liquid refreshed as it slid down her throat.

Seeing her abductor's face again had brought up painful memories. She was exhausted. Her mind was spent, her body drained. She calculated how long it had been since she'd slept. Her body screamed *too long.*

Sadie leaned her head back and closed her eyes.

After a good soak in the tub, she washed herself before stepping out and hand-washing her clothes in the sink. The shower rod was as good a place as any to hang her garments to dry, so she did.

There was toothpaste on the counter. She squeezed some from the tube and finger-brushed her teeth. It was better than nothing. She tightened the towel around her, and moved into the hall, closing the door to the bathroom behind her.

Nick sat on the couch, flipping through TV channels. He did a double take when she stepped into the room wearing only a towel.

She stopped in the living room, completely aware of how naked she was underneath the towel. His reaction had set off a small fire inside her.

"You, uh, want to sit down?"

If she wasn't so tired, she would've experienced a thrill that her femininity seemed to rob his ability to speak clearly. "Okay."

She curled up on the other end of the sofa.

"You want the remote?" He held it out toward her, but his gaze didn't leave hers. He pushed off the sofa and disappeared into the bedroom, returning a minute later holding a comforter. "This should keep you warm."

The blanket was thick, warm and soft. She pulled it up to her neck and thanked him. "This is perfect."

He stood there for a long moment and raked his fingers through his black-as-night curls. "I, uh, should probably go get cleaned up."

Sensual heat vibrated between them. "I found a towel for you and folded it on the counter."

He double-checked the locks on the window in the living room and kitchen. "You want this?" He held out his weapon.

The sight of a gun sent her body into a full-on shiver. "Yeah. I should be prepared. Just in case."

"No one will find us here. I trust Paul. No one in the agency knows about him." He hesitated outside the bathroom door. "I won't be long. You need anything, yell. I'll be here in a snap."

The image of him naked, wet, muscled, lit another small fire. Combine the two and the blaze could get out of control quickly.

True to his word, he wasn't ten minutes in the shower. He strolled into the living room with a towel secured around his hips. Beads of water trailed down his muscular chest.

Now it was Sadie's turn to flush.

"Found these." He held up toothbrushes still in their wrappers.

She turned off the cooking show she'd been watching and joined him next to the sink in the bathroom.

He handed one over, and she opened it immediately, put toothpaste on it and scrubbed her teeth. "This is heaven."

They hovered over the sink, their heads so close they almost touched as they took turns under the faucet.

"I can throw your clothes in the wash with mine." He picked up his jeans and shirt.

"You found a washer?"

"In the hallway leading to the bedrooms."

"Wouldn't hurt to run them through a cycle." She made her way back to the sofa as he turned on the washer. Was there anything sexier than a half-naked man who knew how to take care of himself and everyone around him?

She didn't think so. She couldn't imagine Tom washing his own clothes. Everything had to be sorted by color, placed in the correct bins and dropped off at the cleaners who knew exactly how he liked his things washed and pressed. She was almost embarrassed to remember that he had his summer shorts ironed. He had good qualities, she reminded herself. Manly? Not so much.

Nick, who was nothing but all-man and muscle and smart, walked into the room. Her gaze dipped to his towel and the line of hair from his navel to…the trail ended at his towel. His raw sensual appeal lit another little fire.

"You can change the channel if you want. There wasn't much on earlier excerpt for crime shows."

"I don't mind watching whatever." He settled next to her. His thigh touched hers and the power of that one touch ignited little blazes all down her leg.

She pulled the blanket over her and turned the cooking show back on.

"Want to share?"

His gaze intensified on the screen. "I'm, uh, okay."

Did he feel it, too?

He must have. He'd never had so much trouble putting together a string of words before. Another trill of excitement rushed through her at the thought she had the power to affect such a beautiful man. His body was perfection on a stick. He didn't seem to realize or care, and that just made him even sexier.

He put his arm around her, and she settled into the hollow of his neck. His body radiated warmth.

It would be a mistake to get too comfortable in his arms. The reasons were clipped onto the waistband of his jeans most of the time. His gun. His badge.

Two excellent reasons to keep her emotions under control and not fall into the trap of thinking this could be any more than what it was right then.

Nick was her handler.

It was his job to protect her.

Making her feel safe was part of his assignment. Making her feel sexy wasn't. He stirred another part of her she shouldn't allow.

Sadie didn't want to think about that tonight.

The cooking host sliced an onion in half, running the blade through each side again and again until it was chopped.

The sounds from the TV in the background couldn't drown out the beating of Nick's heart.

She burrowed deeper into the crook of his arm and closed her eyes.

Chapter Fourteen

Sadie woke to the smell of fresh coffee. She sat up and realized she must've dozed off on the couch last night. Naked save for a towel wrapped around her. Embarrassment sent a rash crawling up her neck. She immediately checked to make sure all her body parts were covered.

The blanket still covered her.

Nick sat at a desk that was tucked into the corner of the small dining room. His back was to her, his face toward the screen. She glimpsed cold metal from the waistband of his jeans—a constant reminder he lived in a violent world—one she might never get used to. His job was dangerous.

She pushed the thought aside, preferring not to think about many reasons they would never be able to be a couple. Even though there wasn't exactly an offer of a relationship on the table. The draw she felt to him was unexplainable. Then again, he was one seriously hot guy who was strong to boot. Who wouldn't be attracted to that?

"That coffee I smell?"

He held up a foam cup. She hadn't even heard him get up or go out.

"It is. And good morning to you."

"You didn't happen to buy two of those, did you?"

He turned to face her, and her heart stuttered. His black hair disheveled, stubble on his chin, only made him more irresistible. Damn that he was gorgeous in the morning. In the afternoon. In the evening. Hell, he looked good all the time.

He was also a man with a gun and badge.

"As a matter of fact, I did." He grabbed a small paper bag from the desk and removed another cup. "And I picked up food. Breakfast tacos. I got one with bacon and one with sausage. I wasn't sure which you liked."

Scrambled eggs with cheese, bacon and salsa rolled in a warm tortilla. A Tex-Mex treat she'd grown to love since living in Texas. "That smells amazing. I'm all about the bacon. Definitely bacon. On second thought, this is too good to be true. You're probably just a hallucination, a figment of my overtired imagination. Am I even awake yet?" She blinked, taking the treasures from him. "If I am, I should get dressed."

"It's real." He bent down and kissed her forehead. "I'm real. I happened to like what you're wearing. But if you don't stop looking so damn adorable, you're going to find out just how very real I am."

"Oh."

"So you better distract me by telling me how well you slept last night." He smiled and stroked her cheek.

"Best night of sleep I've had in a long time." The fire he'd lit last night blazed to attention again. She half remembered his body curled behind hers, and the feeling of everything being right in the world while she was nestled against him. She'd never felt like that in another man's arms.

There was something special about Nick.

Did she just blush again? "How about you? Did you get any sleep or did you stay awake all night at that computer?"

"And miss out on feeling your body against mine? Hell, no. I was right there all night." He pointed to the space behind her. "And I slept like a rock."

She took a sip of coffee, welcoming the burn. "Let me guess, job hazard?"

"Yeah. It'd be dangerous for me to let my guard down." His smile tightened. His gaze focused on a square on the carpet.

Based on the change in his expression, she had the very real sense they were about to talk about a heavy subject.

They hadn't finished their conversation from yesterday. He would most likely want to know more about the man in the picture. And what he'd done to her. Her body shuddered, thinking about it. She didn't want to relive the past. She'd much rather stay in the present, the here and now. A primal urge had her wanting to trace the muscles of his back with her finger, follow the patch of hair from his navel down to where his blood pulsed.

First, she'd enjoy her meal. "Have you heard from your family this morning?"

"Luke called first thing. Everyone agreed to check in every few hours until this is over and he's heard from everyone but Lucy. Said she's probably tied up on a case. He says Reed took Boomer out for a run this morning."

"I bet he loved it. I used to take him out back and throw the ball. Half the time he'd end up splashing in the lake. What was supposed to be a quick outing turned into an ordeal. Muddy paws. The smell of lake water. I'd have to give him a bath before I could bring him back inside."

She took a bite of her taco, washing it down with a sip of coffee. The warmth felt good on her throat.

"I'm sure he misses you. I know I would."

The statement made tears prick her eyes. Not being with Nick? Her stomach lurched at the thought. Yet, there would come a time when this case was over and they'd go their separate ways. Her heart squeezed and she couldn't deal with thinking about it right now. "What about the others?"

"Meg and Riley are in Fort Worth with his parents, so they're good. She's started contractions."

"Oh, how exciting for them. They must be thrilled." Thoughts of having a baby tugged at her heart. Would she be around to meet the little one? She hoped so. If not, maybe there could be a special arrangement worked out. "I'm so happy for them both. That's going to be one lucky little kid."

"Yeah, they'll be great parents."

"They sure will. This little one will also be surrounded by an amazing family. I can imagine spending summers out on the ranch with Gran. The place would burst with people on the weekends with cousins, aunts and uncles. And there'd be food everywhere." It was exactly the environment she'd want for her child, if she ever had one.

"I like the sound of that."

His smile warmed her heart.

"For now, they sounded nervous as hell. And my little tough Meg in the background sounded like she was in pain." He chuckled.

"She'll do great. It'll all be worth it when she holds that baby in her arms."

"Doc says a first labor can go on for days before the baby comes." He shrugged. "I'll make sure and check in with Meg later. Almost forgot. Luke said the last time he spoke to Lucy she said there's some big news about her and Stephen but they won't say what it is until we're all under the same roof and can celebrate together."

"Are you thinking what I'm thinking?" She took another sip of coffee anticipation lightening her heavy heart.

"I'm guessing they're announcing an engagement."

Sadie was genuinely happy for Lucy. "I hope so. He did say it was good news, right?"

Luke's smile reached his eyes that time. "Yeah. They also said it was scary. Marriage can seem that way. So I've heard."

His brown eyes sparkled. He got that glittery look of pride every time he talked about his family. His love for them was written all over the sappy smile on his face and the pride in his eyes. His smile might be sentimental, but the way those lips curled at the corners was sexy, too.

She didn't want to ruin his mood, or make him think about the past but curiosity was getting the best of her. "What about you? Ever have any plans to take the leap with anyone?"

NICK COULDN'T EXACTLY pinpoint why he wanted to tell Sadie about his past, but he did. Whatever the hell it was, it must be the same driving force making him want to share details about his family. Something he rarely ever did with anyone. "Yeah. There was someone once. It was a long time ago."

"Do you mind if I ask what happened?" She offered him her coffee.

"No. Ask me anything." He paused long enough to take a sip and hand her cup back to her. "I was young. Thought I had life all figured out. What did I know? She and I had been going together for years already."

"Was she your high-school sweetheart?"

"How'd you know that?"

"I hope you don't mind. Lucy told me a little bit about her."

"Lucy is the most protective of me. I'm surprised she told you anything. She's the quiet one in the family."

"I sensed you two were close. She told me about what happened to her."

A set of surprised eyes stared at her. "That she told you anything about me is shocking. I have no words for her telling you about what happened to her. I can tell you this, though—when that bastard hurt her, I nearly lost my mind. I wanted to kill him with my bare hands."

"If I'm being honest, I'm surprised you didn't. Your family stopped you?"

Tension had him grinding his back teeth. "Thankfully. When he went to trial, I sat in the courtroom and listened to his testimony. All I could do was sit there, helpless, trying to figure out how many punches I could get in before the bailiff could pull me off him."

"But you didn't."

"Not with Gran sitting next to me, holding on to my arm. She knew exactly what I was thinking."

"I've said it before and I'll say it again. Smart woman."

"It almost killed me to let the courts handle him. I was young and angry. The world pissed me off, and I was ready to take out my frustration."

"What happened?"

"I signed up for the military, ready and willing to fight just about anyone. Rachael didn't want me to go to war. She wanted me to go away to school with her."

"But you didn't."

He intensely focused on the patch of carpet at his feet. "Nothing like nonstop fighting for four years to screw your head back on straight. Before my tour was up, I'd planned to ask her to marry me. I'd sent money home to help Mom and Gran take care of the others. I had a little tucked away for college. Rachael wasn't thrilled I didn't listen to her before, but I thought we had it worked out. She had no idea I was about to surprise her with a ring."

"And then…"

"We argued about where the relationship was going. She decided to party with her friends on New Year's Eve instead of spending it with me. A drunk driver crossed the median and hit her car head-on."

"I'm so sorry."

"The crazy thing was I'd had that ring in my pocket for a year. For some reason, I didn't ask. I held on to it. Even though she'd made it clear she wanted me to. Guess I thought I had plenty of time. Or maybe I had my doubts about taking the plunge. Marriage seemed so perma-nent. When I finally realized I wanted to ask, I wanted everything to be perfect. Maybe make up for not asking before. I had it all planned out. I was going to ask first thing New Year's Day…"

He heard Sadie mumble a few words meant to comfort him, like *I'm sorry,* and *Life can be so unfair.*

This was the first time he'd spoken about Rachael with anyone outside of his family. Hell, he didn't say much to his family about the topic.

God, it felt good to finally talk about it. To get it off his chest. He'd been holding everything in for so long, erecting an impenetrable barrier around his heart.

Sadie got up, stood in front of him, her arms around him. He leaned forward, resting his forehead on her stom-ach, holding on to her around her waist.

"I can't help thinking if I'd asked her sooner, somehow things would have turned out differently."

"You don't have a crystal ball."

He still felt the burden of wishing he could go back and change the past. "My timing sucked."

"You couldn't have known what would happen."

"Maybe if I'd asked her the night before, she would've been with my family celebrating instead of going out with her friends."

"That might not have changed the outcome."

He clenched his fists. "Yeah, well I'll never know now. I could've been the one to run into her for how responsible I felt after."

"It wasn't your fault."

Those four words were more effective than a bullet, piercing the Kevlar encasing his heart.

He sat up, keeping his gaze on hers the entire time, waiting, expecting her to tell him to stop or give him a signal this couldn't happen.

Instead, her tongue slicked across her lips and he couldn't tear his gaze away from the silky trail.

"Do that again and I won't be able to stop myself from doing things I'm not convinced you're ready for."

He could see her heartbeat at the base of her throat. It took everything in him not to lean forward and press his lips there.

"You didn't try to kiss me last night. I thought you'd changed your mind about making love to me."

Damn, she was sexy with her big green glittery eyes staring at him. "I don't flip-flop. I just wanted you to be sure you're ready for this—this changes things between us."

"Are you telling me you've never had sex for sex's sake before?"

"Sure, when I was young and stupid. I'm a grown man now, and I like to know I'll be welcome back before I go down that road. I don't do one night."

"I like the sound of that."

"Then make sure you're good and awake because I want full awareness for what I plan to do to you."

She sucked in a little burst of air. "Hold that thought."

She disappeared down the hallway, and he could hear the sink water running in the bathroom and the swish of her toothbrush.

He clasped his hands together and rested his elbows on his knees. The debate about whether or not this was a good idea was a lost argument at this point.

Nick wanted Sadie more than he needed air.

His pulse hummed when he saw Sadie standing there. Her wavy brown hair layered around her shoulders, wearing nothing but a towel wrapped around her and tied at the top.

"You want me, Nick?"

His chest hurt for how bad he needed to be inside her. His erection was already painfully stiff. "I think you already know the answer to that question."

"Then I'm all yours." She untied the knot in one quick motion, and the towel pooled at her feet.

Chapter Fifteen

The pure beauty of her body, her sensuous curves, kept him rooted to his spot as she walked toward him. Her gaze never left his as she walked him to the couch and nudged him to sit down.

She stood in front of him then gripped his shoulders and pushed until he pressed against the backrest. "Dammit, Sadie. Are you determined to finish this before it gets started?"

She grinned, looking as if she understood and enjoyed the effect she had on him. "Something wrong?"

"Abso-freakin-lutely-not. Everything in my view couldn't be more perfect. But I do want this to last and you're making that very difficult for me."

She straddled him. "How about now?"

"Heaven." He gripped her waist as she rocked back and forth, fighting the urge to drive himself inside her. He needed to remove his jeans, but she felt so damn incredible, he didn't want to move. Plus, truth be told, he liked allowing her to set the pace.

She leaned forward, her bare breasts skimming his chest, and he breathed in her floral soap scent.

The image of her in those boots, wearing jeans and her pale pink sweater, broke through his thoughts. He'd been wanting, no needing to touch her ever since that moment in his truck. Hell, if he was being honest, ever since that first day he'd met her at the bakery.

He smoothed his palm over her flat stomach, and then wrapped it around her sweet bottom. Electric impulse drilled through him. The need to be inside her caused an ache in his chest.

Patience.

"You're an amazing woman, Sadie," he whispered, "and incredibly beautiful."

A pink flush rose to her cheeks. Her green eyes darkened. Desire. "Then make love to me."

Better-sounding words had never crossed those pink lips in the time he'd known her.

He pressed a kiss to the hollow of her neck. Then, he lowered his head to her breastbone and feathered kisses there, making his way down to her pert breasts.

Kissing the tip of her breast, he slid his tongue up to her neck. He feathered a kiss on the small mole on her cheek. He found her mouth and groaned when she teased his tongue into her mouth. She nipped his bottom lip.

Little did she know, it was her turn to squirm. He slid his tongue in her mouth. He palmed her breast. With his other hand, he drew circles on her sex.

She moaned.

He pulled and tugged at her pointed peak.

Her eyes opened and the power of that one look almost knocked him back. She didn't need words to tell him she wanted him inside her. Right then.

"Patience."

Her cheeks were flush as he gripped the dimpled spot above her sweet bottom.

With her naked and warm body pressed up against him, he realized just how perfectly she fit him.

The feel of her bare, clean skin was enough to drive him to the brink even with his jeans on.

But he would force himself to wait, to savor every second of this until passion couldn't be held at bay anymore.

He thrust his tongue deep in her mouth, needing to taste every inch of her. She returned the intensity of his kiss.

With one arm wrapped around her waist, he pulled her body in tight against his until her heat pressed against his stomach. His hands wandered over every inch of her stomach until they rose to her full breasts. Her skin was soft.

Her wet heat was so close to his erection, his body hummed.

Patience.

He pushed up enough to sit, picked her up and carried her into the next room, where he placed her on the bed and dipped down to kiss her. She gripped his neck and pulled him on top of her.

He trailed kisses down her neck until his mouth found her breasts, roaming, as the tip of his tongue flicked the crest of her nipple before taking it in his mouth.

She moaned and gripped his shoulders.

"Just a minute," he said. His hands went to the button on his jeans, but her hands were already there, hungry, tearing button by button. Damn, he got so caught up in the moment, he almost forgot something. "Hold that thought."

He retrieved a condom from the wallet in his back pocket, then let his jeans drop to the floor.

"This is insane. I've never been with a more beautiful woman." With both knees on the bed, he leaned forward and his lips crushed down on hers.

He broke free long enough to rip open the condom

package. Her hands were already around his shaft as he rolled the condom over his tip and moaned as she stroked him.

"I want you. Now."

"Then take me," she said. Her hands were on him again. Her fingers traced his jawline, down his chin, along his Adam's apple. "I have never wanted a man like I want you right now."

He eased her onto the bed. Before he could make another move, her legs wrapped around his midsection. He tensed as she guided him inside her.

He thrust, her body taking him in, and his control nearly shattered. He plunged deep inside her again and again, slowing his pace every time he neared the edge.

She greedily clutched at his back, pulling him deeper into her as their bodies molded together.

He thrust. Surged.

When her muscles clenched, released, exploded around him, he pumped harder as she bucked her hips and said his name over and over until he detonated.

He collapsed on top of her, careful not to overwhelm her with his weight, needing to stay inside her, with her, in this moment, for as long as he could.

NICK'S BODY STILL glistened with beads of water when he returned from the shower with nothing but a towel wrapped around his waist.

His cell buzzed. He located his jeans and retrieved it from his front pocket. "It's Meg."

"You better take the call." She patted the seat next to her, reaching out for his free hand.

He twined their fingers and took a seat.

"How's she doing?" He asked into the phone. His gaze locked on to Sadie's. "It's Riley."

She nodded.

"How far apart?"

"Fifteen minutes," Riley said.

He heard Meg in the background groaning and clamped his back teeth. "And the doctor doesn't think she should go to the hospital yet?"

"We're leaving my parents' house now. I don't care what the doctor says. Fort Worth is a long drive from Plano."

"Which hospital?"

"Presby."

Nick glanced at his watch. This time of morning traffic shouldn't be too bad. "I can be there in twenty minutes."

"I'll meet you there."

"Okay, man. Meg is saying she doesn't want you to come."

"Did I say I was planning on asking permission? Besides, what she doesn't know won't hurt her."

"Feel free to take your life in your own hands." Riley chuckled. "I'll call you as soon as we get there."

"Hell, I'll be waiting at the front door."

Sadie squeezed his hand before disappearing into the other room.

He presumed to get dressed. He could think of a few things he would've liked to have done while she was still almost naked on the couch. His hormones were overriding rational thought again.

When it came to Sadie, he had little control over either.

He ended the call with his brother-in-law.

Could he and Sadie have a future when this was all over? The very real notion she had a U.S. Marshal whose career, hell, life, depended on her not being alive to identify him pressed down on Nick.

Sadie stepped across the hall and he could see that she'd put clothes on and left the bathroom door open as she brushed her teeth.

If Nick could protect her, he might just be able to think about having a relationship with her. Or could he? She was scared to death of his constant companion, his Glock, and he wore a badge. The very badge he loved also prevented him from getting involved personally with her.

And yet, she'd broken through the shield protecting his heart. She'd cracked the armor…and he couldn't say he was especially sorry.

Chapter Sixteen

"Change of plans today. I picked up a few supplies when I was out. Put these on." Nick held out a sweatshirt, wig and sunglasses. "Meg and Riley are on their way to the hospital."

"That's so exciting." Sadie tried on the black cropped hair, tugging at the sides until it felt right. "How do I look?"

He grinned, wrapped his arms around her waist and kissed the hollow of her neck. "Not bad."

He thrust his hips forward and she could feel his arousal.

Need welled deep inside her.

"I don't think you should start something you can't finish," she teased, enjoying the feel of his lips on her skin.

"You're probably right, but I wouldn't mind trying." His sexy smile tore at her heart. And her better judgment. Memories of those lips taunting and teasing other places on her body warmed her. And the feel of his arms around her. She could get used to him. Dangerous thinking for a woman who wanted a peaceful life in the country. No guns. No scary men. No hiding. And yet, he made her think having kids and a husband might not be such a bad idea someday. Maybe she could get another dog to keep Boomer company, too?

The life that everyone else took for granted made her heart ache for how badly she wanted it. Kids, a husband… a stable life were a world away.

A painful stab, like a bullet piercing bone, slammed into her ribs.

Seriously? Hadn't she learned to protect her heart any better than that? If her own family constantly disappointed her, wouldn't Nick do the same? She thought she'd gotten pretty darn good at keeping everyone at a safe distance. But here she was falling hard for Nick. The icing on the cake was that he wore a gun for a living.

Didn't she have any more sense than to fall in love with a man whose job would ensure many late nights of her wide awake worrying about him? A lifetime of fear?

And, yet, looking into those cinnamon, copperlike eyes melted her reserves every time.

They'd had incredibly hot sex. She couldn't argue that. Clearly, the bedroom would not be a problem for them.

But most of life was lived outside the sheets.

The big question would be did they have what it takes to make a relationship work with their clothes on? Or would two very important pieces of equipment get in the way? A badge and a gun.

She already knew the answer. Her body shook every time she was near either one.

What if he left the Marshals Service and got another job? a little voice inside her head asked.

And take away everything that was Nick?

No way would she ask. He was too good at what he did to think about him in another line of work. He saved innocent people. She would never be so selfish as to ask him to change.

She straightened her wig. "Ready?"

He groaned, nuzzling his face in her neck. "Just give me another minute."

"Okay, but you might miss the birth of one very important little person."

"You're beautiful when you're right." He skimmed his lips across her collarbone. "And you're sexy when you're thinking about others." He feathered kisses where her heart beat at the base of her throat. "And especially when you're looking out for me." His lips found hers, and he pressed a sweet kiss to her mouth.

She wanted to dissolve in his arms.

Bad idea.

He'd regret not being there for Meg.

"Keep this up and we won't get out of here," she said.

He grumbled, mumbled a curse word and pulled back. "We'll get back to this later."

"I'm planning to hold you to your word." She returned his smile.

"You, a couple of steaks on the grill, a cold beer and I might never want to leave." He finished getting dressed. He dipped his head under the running faucet to wet his hair then finger-combed it. He put on a ball cap and shades.

Her heart stuttered.

This was the Nick she remembered from the bakery.

The one who'd first piqued her interest.

"Heard from Lucy yet?"

"No. I left her a voice mail. I'll check in with Luke once we get to the hospital."

Sadie slid her feet into her boots. She should hate them by now. Her heels might never recover from the blisters. But the hard leather was beginning to give. She was starting to wear them in and, heck, they were too awesome

not to adore. They fit her to a T. Once the leather was
worn in, the blisters would go away, too. She could definitely see herself becoming a Texan when this whole ordeal was behind her. Okay, she'd learned "real" Texans
were Texas-born, but she could be a transplant. One of
those people who may not have been born in Texas but
got there as fast as they could.

Nick put on his shoes, twined their fingers and led her
outside to the truck parked on the pad out front.

Sadie glanced down the street, her usual habit, checking for anything or anyone that looked out of place.
Would there ever come a time when she didn't instinctively do this?

Two years of training had her watching shadows,
checking cars and searching strangers' faces.

At a house four doors down there looked to be someone in the driver's seat of a small blue sport-utility. Could
be nothing. A friend waiting outside for someone to run
inside their house and grab something they'd forgotten.

Being snatched from the grocery store parking lot two
years ago had taught Sadie to fear what was out in the
open more than anything in the dark.

She squeezed Nick's hand and inclined her head toward the parked vehicle. "Think we need to be worried?"

"I saw that. We'll keep an eye on him," he reassured.

Traffic on Interstate 75 was almost at a crawl, but
picked up once they merged onto President George Bush
Turnpike, heading west. Nick took the Dallas North Toll-
way exit, heading north to Parker Road. Once he exited
there, he made a left. A small white building came up
quickly on the left. To the right was a strip mall. Beyond
those, the three towers that made up Texas Health Pres-
byterian Hospital of Plano stood on the left.

"Did they say which tower?"

"The second, I believe."

He pulled into the parking garage and found a parking spot on the third floor.

"Doesn't seem like we had any company on the way." Thankfully, no blue sport-utility had followed them.

"Nope."

And, yet, Sadie had an uneasy feeling.

"You don't look relieved."

Most likely her alert system was set to high beam again. "It's probably nothing."

"Gut instinct has kept me alive more than once." Nick scanned the parking garage as they walked toward the white building.

An ambulance, sirens blazing, roared toward the emergency entrance.

Sadie's nerves were already stretched to their limits. The blare of the sirens caused her muscles to pull tighter with each step toward the elevator.

She caught herself judging every person who passed by, evaluating their threat. Being outside in daylight had her feeling vulnerable even though she wore a disguise.

Nick squeezed her hand reassuringly as they walked inside the building and to the elevators. He seemed to second-guess himself when he glanced at a metal door with a sign over it that read Stairs. "Let's take those instead."

"What floor are they on?"

"The third." He pulled out his phone and thumbed through his texts as the metal door *cu-clunked* behind them. He stalled on the first step. "She's in room three-fifteen."

They'd climbed one set of stairs when Nick's cell buzzed, indicating a text. He checked the screen. "It's from Riley."

Sadie's pulse increased. "What did he say?"

His eyes stayed on the screen for a long moment as though he needed a second for the words to sink in. He muttered a curse. "Men are in the room asking questions about me and he doesn't like it."

"What? How can that be?"

"Riley's telling us to get out of here." His jaw clenched.

"Wait a minute. Isn't this the break we need? Shouldn't we call the police? Have them arrested? Or at least hauled in for questioning?"

"For what?" He paused. "Asking questions in a hospital? If these guys are flashing badges, then local police aren't going to touch them."

"What about the envelope we found in the warehouse last night?"

"Inadmissible in court. We could go to jail for breaking and entering."

"Oh, right. I forgot."

"I need to check in with Smith. Let him know what's happening. And he damn well better be prepared to send extra resources to make sure nothing happens to my family."

He'd already turned around and started back down the stairwell when the door to the first floor flew open. He froze and ended the call before Smith could answer, biting out another curse word under his breath—the exact one Sadie was thinking.

Sadie followed Nick up the stairs as quietly as she could, fearing the people below would hear her heartbeat for how loud it hammered against her ribs.

She heard the unmistakable click of a bullet being loaded in a chamber. She bit down a gasp, staying as close to Nick as she could manage as he ascended the stairs.

Feet shuffled below, climbing closer. By the sounds of it, someone was in a hurry.

She and Nick had two floors on whoever was chasing them, but they were gaining ground fast.

Nick popped out on the seventh floor and immediately pressed the elevator button.

Hurry.

The elevator dinged and a set of doors opened. Nick rushed inside. "Get against the wall."

She pressed her back against the glass, saying a silent protection prayer.

The stairwell door flung open.

"This where they ditched?" a familiar-sounding voice asked. Did it belong to Burly?

Nick jammed his thumb on the L button a few more times.

Come on.

"I don't think so. I don't see anyone. Maybe one up?" another voice replied. Steroids?

The elevator door closed at the same time as the one leading to the stairs.

"You know who that was, don't you?" she asked.

"I do. They sure have come a long way from the cabin to find us," he said, staring at the screen on his phone intently.

"My thinking exactly. Is it possibly they work for the agency?"

"No. I'd know if they did. Those guys are hired."

She gasped. "You mean professional killers?"

He nodded. "We need to get to my truck and I need to get ahold of Smith. But I want to see who else comes out of the front door before we leave."

The elevator stopped at the second floor. Sadie's heart lurched to her throat.

Nick drew his weapon, and hid it behind his leg. Sadie went shoulder-to-shoulder with him, frighteningly aware of how close the gun was to her own leg, in order to shield the weapon from view. Her body started to shake.

Four or five people pushed in before the elevator doors closed again. A man in scrubs, two nurses and an older couple squeezed inside, making the small space cramped.

The lobby was a welcomed sight.

Nick walked quickly the few steps away from the elevator then broke into a run, not stopping until he was out the front door. He walked across the pathway to an uncovered parking lot and phoned Smith.

"Meg's in the hospital getting ready to have her baby. She had visitors. I need people on her, Smith. My life is one thing, but keep my sister safe."

Sadie only heard one side of the conversation, mostly Nick stressing the need to provide adequate protection for his family.

He asked his boss to hold then checked a text message. "My brother-in-law says the men who stopped by gave names. They also claimed to be coworkers of mine."

By the time he closed the call, he'd relayed the message whoever visited Meg claimed to work with him said their names were Young and Turner.

Based on Nick's reaction, those identities didn't sit well with his boss.

"What did he say?" she asked as soon as Nick looked at her.

"It's impossible for Young and Turner to be here because they're on assignment in Virginia."

"He's sure they're there? I mean couldn't they say they were in one place but actually hop a plane and be here in a few hours?"

"Yeah." His gaze constantly shifted, scanning for possible threats. "But they didn't."

"What makes him so certain? I mean it's not as if

someone follows you guys around checking out your every move."

"He knew because he'd just left them at breakfast. They had a meeting about the case they were working on. No way could they eat with him then make it here in an hour."

"Then clearly someone is getting away with impersonating marshals. How can that happen?"

"Jamison would have access to everyone's personnel records. All he'd have to do is find men who looked similar and then have their credentials faked."

"And his association with Grimes would give him access to a variety of known criminals and channels. Men who would be good at pretending to be someone else when they needed to. Men who could fake government documents skillfully."

"Men who wouldn't be afraid to kill someone to get what they wanted." He finished for her.

Shock wasn't the word for what Sadie experienced. "Isn't it pretty brazen of them to come to the hospital like this? I mean they have to know Meg and Riley are cops."

"Why not? They've already gone to prison and fooled guards. Killed a U.S. Marshal. They're good at this and clearly comfortable with what they're doing."

"What did Riley say to them?"

"He told them I was driving in from Houston, and that I'd be there in two hours. He also asked them to stick around. He said they couldn't get out of there fast enough. He had no reason to detain them, so he had to let them go."

"Not to mention his wife's in labor, and he has no backup." Sadie pointed out.

"Even so, he would've done anything necessary to keep her safe. Even if that meant placing them under arrest."

"What was Smith's reaction to the news?"

"He has extra security coming. I'd like to stick around in case Riley needs me until they arrive." Stress gave way to a long face.

"I hate that you can't be there for Meg while she's in labor."

"Me, too. At least she has Riley with her. He said she probably wouldn't let me come inside, anyway. Something about not wanting to scare me off ever having children." His smile didn't look forced, but faded quickly.

"Who are we looking for?"

"For one, I'd like to know more about the two men who seem to be behind us every step of the way." He checked his messages. "Then there's the pair of men wearing dark suits. Riley said they should stick out."

Sadie studied each person as they came out of the turnstiles.

Five minutes passed before anyone fitting the description came out of the revolving doors of the main building.

"Looks like we have them." Nick switched his phone to camera mode and snapped a couple of pictures. "I'll send these to Smith, and we'll hope for a positive ID."

"You think they might be deputies?"

"Could be. If Jamison sent them and they're following his orders then it's possible they might not even know what he's really after. If they're known criminals, they'll show up in the database, and we'll get a hit." He sent the photos to his boss with a couple of clicks.

"We haven't seen Burly and Steroids. Where could they have possibly gone?"

"It's a big building with multiple exits. They could've gone out somewhere else, and we'd never know. Or they could be in the building. I should warn Riley." He fired off a text to his brother-in-law.

"Can't he detain those guys?"

"He needs to have probable cause." He studied the screen intently.

"Any word from Smith?"

"Not yet. It could take a while to get a match."

"Should we wait here for backup?"

"Let's see where these guys go first. We might want to follow them. At least get a good look at the license plate."

The men walked to a white sedan.

Nick repositioned. "Damn. I can't get a good look at the plate. Too many cars in the way."

He crouched low and moved behind another car, trying to get a better position.

Sadie saw a man in white shirt and black pants heading toward them. "Security's coming."

The radio squawked.

"Keep an eye on him." He moved up another couple of cars.

"He's heading right this way, Nick."

He dropped to his knees and fanned his hands out on the ground, feeling around. "Can you see them, babe?"

"Looking for something, sir?" the guard looked concerned.

"My keys." He felt around underneath a different car. "Dropped them."

The security officer bent down, placing his hands on his knees for support. He had to be close to fifty, and his belly prevented him from bending too far.

Sadie pointed toward the key Nick had dropped moments before. "That it?"

"Where?" He played the part perfectly.

"There. Near the grass by the front tire."

"Look at that. Sure is."

The officer stood to his full height, which looked to be five-foot-ten, as Nick rose to his and offered to shake hands.

"I'd be lost without her."

The officer smiled and nodded, shaking his head and walking toward the building. "I wouldn't be caught dead admitting that to mine. She'd never let me hear the end of it. But it's true."

Sadie turned in time to see the white sedan turn the corner onto Communications Parkway and disappear.

Nick muttered a curse. "You didn't happen to get that number, did you?"

"Nope. I didn't. And we wouldn't be able to catch them at this point, either, would we?"

He grumbled while he shook his head. "Not even if we ran to the truck. Besides, being in a hurry might cause us to make a mistake and be seen. Burly and Steroids might still be in the building."

It was most likely her danger radar overreacting again, but she didn't like the thought of those men being anywhere near Nick's pregnant sister.

This situation couldn't get more frustrating to Nick. If they went inside, where he wanted to be to watch over his sister, they risked Burly and Steroids seeing him. Jamison's camp had been led to believe Nick was nowhere around. His henchmen would be expecting him and Sadie to be on Interstate 45 heading north. They would most likely put some resources there.

Riley's knee-jerk reaction to throw them off the trail had been brilliant. Jamison wouldn't be happy waiting

around for Nick to show up at the hospital. He'd send resources to cut him off and dispose of him long before he
had a chance to make it to Plano. Jamison's life depended
on getting rid of Nick and Sadie.

Spreading out Jamison's men improved Nick's odds
greatly.

He pulled his cell from his pocket and informed Smith,
so he could put resources on I-45. In exchange, he learned
support should be arriving at the hospital any second.

Glancing at Sadie, he could see how stressed this situation had been on her. He wanted to reach out to her,
to be her comfort, to take all her fear and anxiety away.

He hated that he couldn't.

Another part of him wanted to find Burly and Steroids, if only to force them to talk. He had a few other
ideas of things he'd like to do to them, but jail sounded
like a good enough option.

Leaving Sadie alone so he could track them was a
bad idea.

Bringing her along wasn't an option.

He had no doubt if he was alone he would find them
if they were still in the building. Two people would be
harder to hide.

Sitting and waiting was a bitter cup of tea for Nick.

Yet, that was what he had to do.

Once he knew Meg, Riley and baby were safe, he
could leave. Stashing Sadie at the safe house was his
best bet until he heard back from Smith. His men were
zeroing in on Jamison, and it wouldn't be long before
they had a location.

Until then, Nick would be better off in hiding, too.

The last thing he wanted to do was lead Jamison to
Sadie. She was the only one who could identify him as

one of her abductors. They needed her statement against Jamison to be able to make an arrest. He had another more personal reason for keeping Sadie safe, but this was not the time to get inside his head about what that meant.

Without proof, Jamison would most likely get off scot-free if Nick and Sadie were killed. She was the only person who could identify him and put him away.

It was bad enough they had to deal with an out-of-control marshal, but Grimes was another story. He had a vested interest in seeing Sadie dead, too. He also seemed hell-bent on making sure she was erased for good. Dead would do it.

Nick's cell buzzed. Smith's name popped up on the screen. He showed it to Sadie before answering. "What's the word, Chief?"

"My men have arrived. It's safe for you and 'the battery' to leave." The boss must've realized Nick wouldn't leave the grounds until he knew his sister was out of danger.

"I appreciate this. You'll keep someone here until she checks out in a couple of days?"

"I'll send someone home with them if it means you won't worry. They'll have twenty-four-hour security. You have enough on your plate right now without wondering if your family's safe."

"What next?"

"I'm in the process of trying to attain a search warrant for Jamison's house. Sadie's word and the bank account might just be enough."

"Jamison lives in Dallas, I presume."

"Right."

Nick would like to be part of the guys serving that warrant, but he suspected the place would be empty.

"He's smart enough to know better than to hide evidence at his house."

"I suspect you're right."

"Doesn't hurt to take a look, anyway," Nick conceded. "Keep me in the loop."

"You know I will."

Nick ended the call. "Back to the safe house."

Waiting made him want to go insane. He also wasn't thrilled by the fact he hadn't heard from Lucy.

He could see fear in Sadie's eyes when she looked at him and nodded. His muscles tensed. She shouldn't have to hide for the rest of her life. Just thinking about how afraid she'd been—how afraid she'd most likely be forever—stirred anger that pierced another hole in his armor.

Grimes needed to be behind bars. Jamison especially needed to be in a cell. And there were a few things he wanted to do to the both of them first that he was sure the agency wouldn't approve. And, yet, if he got his bare hands near them, he'd make sure they knew he'd been there.

He needed to tuck Sadie away until they found Jamison and made sure he couldn't hurt anyone again.

Sadie was quiet on the drive back to the safe house. Nick could feel fear radiating from her. He occasionally reached over to squeeze her hand, to reassure her.

He told her everything would be okay and that they'd find them first.

What he refused to tell her was that this had just become a high stakes game of hide-and-seek…and both of their lives depended on not being found first.

Chapter Seventeen

Nick pulled onto the parking pad with the ever-present feeling of eyes watching him. His instincts didn't normally lead him down the wrong path, so he didn't ignore them.

Yet, scanning the houses, yards and vehicles parked on the street didn't reveal anything out of the ordinary. Kids were still in school, so the streets were quiet.

The winds had kicked up, typical late-November weather. It was noon but the clouds rolling in covered the sun, making it feel more like nightfall. In six hours, the sky would already be dark this time of year.

"Think it's going to rain?"

He shrugged as he exited the cab. "Never can be sure with Texas weather."

"One minute the sun's shining, the next it can be raining. I'd heard about the storms that come this time of year and how the wide skies open up and pour rain. The thunder that cracks right in your ear."

"I never minded a big storm. We can always use the rain." He caught a glimpse of something moving out of the corner of his eyes. He quickly moved next to Sadie, and realized, for the first time, she was trembling. Anger hit him faster than a bolt of lightning.

He put his body between her and whatever had

moved. Might be nothing, but he knew better than to take chances.

Unlocking the front door, he urged Sadie inside. If someone knew where the safe house was, they could be waiting inside. He thought about the blue sport-utility that had been parked a few doors down earlier. He glanced over his shoulder in the general direction where it had been parked. The vehicle was gone.

Was it a coincidence?

Instinct told him not to take anything for granted.

Once inside, he hauled Sadie behind him and drew his gun. He leveled his weapon in front of him.

The lights were off. Without sunlight filtering in through the windows, the place was dark.

He had to take into account the possibility that Paul's relatives had come home early. The scenario was unlikely but had to be considered. "This is Marshal Campbell."

No one responded.

If someone was in the house, they didn't want to be found. Not yet.

Sadie's body shook from fear and probably cold, since the temperature had dropped twenty degrees in the past hour, and they didn't have coats.

With her pressed against his back, he felt every rigid muscle in her body. Everything in him wanted to take away that feeling for her. Make it go away forever.

From his vantage point at the front door, he could see the living room, kitchen and dining room. He swept the area. No surprises there.

The bathroom and pair of bedrooms yielded similar results. The laundry room in the hallway was clear.

Now to assess any threat outside.

He could leave Sadie inside where he was relatively sure she'd be safe. Or risk taking her outside with him.

Leaving her alone could be exactly what Jamison or Grimes would want. Could someone be setting a trap?

On balance, bringing Sadie was a risk he had to take.

Nick moved to the big window in the living room, leaving the lights off.

He peered outside and waited. *Patience.*

A text came through. Everyone had checked in but Lucy.

Movement around the back of Luke's truck caught his attention.

This was no coincidence.

"Stay behind me. Don't move unless I do."

Her eyes were wide, but she nodded.

He moved to the door leading to the small backyard. There was enough of a glow from the lamps across the alley for him to see lines for clothes and winter melon plantings that led from the house to the back fence. The gate was on the opposite side of the house as the parking pad. Nick slid outside with Sadie practically glued to his back.

Gusts of winds blasted, sending leaves thrashing through the air. Tree branches bent and snapped. A big storm was brewing.

Nick dropped down on all fours and crawled toward the front of the house, his shoulder scraping against the building as he moved, urging Sadie to follow along. He stopped at the corner, checking the building next to them, across the street and then behind them.

Rain pelted his face and made it hard to see clearly.

Wind whipped sideways, and a cracking noise split the air. Thunder.

Nick needed to get a visual of the front of the building and see what was going on. With his weapon drawn, he peeked around the building. He was greeted with a spray of bullets.

He planted on his chest, dropping flat on his stomach with Sadie on his heels. He fired a shot toward the figure moving behind the truck as the guy backed away, using the building as cover. His bullet went a little wide and to the right. Between the darkness and the wind, he'd have a difficult time getting off a good shot. *Patience*.

The rustle of someone running toward them came from the yard behind. Stay put and they'd be trapped.

"Listen to me carefully. We're going to have to make a run for it."

Sadie's mouth moved to speak but no words came out. She had been freezing just walking in the house. She had to be in bad shape by now. She'd warm up when she got her blood pumping again. He needed her to move when he gave the signal.

He also knew exactly what she was thinking. "I want you to go first so I can cover you. Once you pop up and get your footing, don't stop running. Got it?"

"Run where?" Panic brought her voice up an octave. To her credit, she fixed her gaze in the direction he pointed.

"Away from the sound of fire."

She nodded.

"On my count. One. Two. Three."

By the time he said the last number, she was to her feet and sprinting across the neighbor's yard.

He covered her, firing a warning shot directly toward the location where bullets had come from.

A figure moved behind the truck, firing one shot after the other. He had to be using a Glock or Beretta or a Sig—there were lots of choices for an automatic—as he dashed toward the tree in the front yard, ducking and rolling to avoid Nick's shot. The guy knew what he was doing. Could it be Jamison?

If so, maybe Nick could end this right there. Arrest him. Put the bastard in jail where he belonged.

Not a chance, a little voice in the back of his head said. Jamison was in too deep. He wouldn't go out willingly. Not after coming this far or going to these lengths to protect his investments. If the supervisor was around, he was there for one purpose. Erase Nick and Sadie.

Nick discharged his weapon again.

The male form used the tree in the front yard as cover. He wasn't running away from anyone, so much as he was running toward Sadie.

Nick heard voices in the backyard. Two, maybe three men were coming from behind. There were too many for Nick to fight off for long, even with his second clip. He was in over his head. He needed to send out a distress call.

Nick fished his phone out of his pocket to call for backup at the same time he heard a shot. Shock overwhelmed him. Was he hit?

He glanced down and saw blood. He made a move to stand, but everything went blurry.

Someone yelled, "Got him!"

Sirens blared.

Could he hide? He belly-crawled toward the vegetable bin he'd spotted earlier. His limbs were weak. His head spun. Where was Sadie? She'd disappeared after she turned the corner around the neighbor's house. Was someone there? Waiting?

No. Couldn't be. She would have screamed. She didn't. And that meant she'd made it to the shops. She could hide there until Nick could find her.

He hauled his heavy frame inside the bin, closing the

lid as he heard footsteps nearing. Another flash of light followed by a crack of thunder sounded overhead.

It was only a matter of time before they would find Nick. He'd left a trail of blood, leading to the bin.

"I saw her turn this way," one of the bastards said. He couldn't be more than five feet from Nick.

His muscles tensed, ready for a fight, then everything went black.

SADIE RAN. HER thighs burned and her lungs clawed for air, but she dragged in another deep breath and pushed forward.

Footsteps were close, closing in, and she had no way to defend herself if the attacker caught up.

Every gunshot blast sent her pulse rocketing into the stratosphere.

"Please, God, let it be Nick behind me." She knew he wasn't there but repeated the prayer, anyway.

There were too many men for Nick to take on by himself.

Thunder cracked, and Sadie let out a yelp before she could squash it.

If someone was behind her, chasing her, wouldn't that mean they'd stopped Nick?

Her mind screamed, *"No!"*

She expected fear to grip her, to paralyze her. Instead, white-hot anger roared through her veins.

If they did anything to Nick, hurt him because they were looking for her...

She wanted to scream.

Maybe she could make it to the strip mall, ditch them and circle back to Nick. The possibility of him lying on the sidewalk, alone, in a pool of his own blood sent anger licking through her veins. If she could get to him—get help—surely paramedics could save him. *Cling to positive thoughts,* she reminded herself. Nick was good at his job. He knew how to handle men like these. He would survive.

She dashed behind one of the houses that backed up to the lot and scrambled up the brick wall separating the neighborhood from retailers.

Nothing bad could happen to Nick. She couldn't allow herself to go there mentally...he would be fine, and they would be together.

If she could get inside one of the stores, she could hide. She still had her cell phone. She could get a message to Smith. He'd send reinforcements. *Stay alive, Nick.*

The reality of him staying back there, alone, to give her a chance to escape pressed down on her chest, making breathing even more difficult. His act of valiance was commendable. Except she couldn't face losing the only man she'd ever loved. Love?

Yeah. Love.

No man had ever made her feel the way he did.

She pushed on.

Rounding the corner to the strip mall, she glanced back in time to see a large man hopping over the brick wall. Not a good sign that he'd gotten past Nick.

Did that mean...?

No.

She refused to think negative thoughts or let fear overtake her. She needed a clear head.

Sadie kept her feet moving forward even though her heart wanted to turn around and find him. He'd said run. He'd told her not to look back. He'd saved her life.

She wouldn't repay him by getting caught if she had anything to say about it.

Turning the last bend to the storefronts, she glanced

across the parking lot. The terra-cotta warriors standing sentinel had men ducking behind them.

She checked behind her. Another minute and the man chasing her would catch up.

Sadie couldn't allow that to happen.

In a sea of black-haired people, she was grateful for the wig. The fact she was a few inches taller than almost everyone else made her easy to spot...not so good.

Luckily, there were lots of shoppers. She pushed through them, keeping as low a profile as she could. When she'd made it past a barbershop and a restaurant, she spotted a supermarket. Perfect.

It was in the middle of the shopping center, but if she could make it there, she could disappear in the aisles. Maybe even slip out the back door, which would lead to the loading dock. She could circle her way back to Nick. He was alive. She refused to think otherwise. He had to be worried about her by now.

Nick was fine. She would find him. They'd get through this.

She'd testify again in a heartbeat if it meant she and Nick could live out the rest of their lives in peace. Maybe even together?

A chest pain so strong it nearly brought her to her knees pierced her.

For a split second, she almost thought she'd been hit by a bullet.

The agony in her chest, she realized, came from knowing deep down that something had happened to Nick.

Otherwise he would be coming for her.

She had to know what happened. What if he lay there, bleeding, and she could help him? Could she get to him in time?

Sirens wailed and her heart stuttered as she made it to the grocery store.

She pulled the cell Nick had given her in Creek Bend from her back pocket. The one she was only supposed to use if he wasn't there—the one she wasn't supposed to need—and hit the only other name in the contacts as she bolted toward the stockroom.

Smith's phone ran into voice mail. "This is Sadie Brooks. We're in trouble…"

A few more steps and she would be able to hide among the boxes of food waiting to be stocked.

A few more steps and she had options.

A few more steps and she could make it to freedom.

Sadie pushed her legs, full force, ignoring the cramp in her calf.

The set of double doors was in reach.

They both flew open at exactly the same time.

There stood Burly.

Chapter Eighteen

Instinct kicked in the moment Burly clamped her in his meaty grip. Sadie wheeled around, trying to break free.

He grinned and tightened his hold on her, forcing her to face him.

She grabbed two fists full of his shirt at chest level, screamed and pivoted her body, sticking her leg out to trip him using his own body weight against him.

He broke into a laugh as he widened his stance. "You think a little thing like you can take me down?"

The leg wheel technique had failed against his two-hundred-plus pounds.

"Help me, somebody," she pleaded.

The small crowd of Asian onlookers dispersed quickly, diverting their gazes away from Sadie.

No one would make eye contact.

Burly hauled her into the stockroom before she could get her mental bearings again. Fists like pit bull jaws locked around her upper arms.

She bent as low as she could, fisted her hands and in one quick motion burst toward the ceiling, breaking free from his hold.

Before he could snatch her again, Sadie wheeled around and exploded toward the metal doors, toward freedom.

Certain she could outrun Burly, hope ballooned in her chest. If she could escape, she could find Nick.

Just shy of reaching the doors, they sprang open.

Steroids.

Sadie screamed a curse as her forward momentum forced her to run smack into his chest. Hopelessness clawed at her. *Not happening. Not again.*

They'd taken away her life before. She'd had to separate from Boomer because of them. They may have killed Nick. She would not go down without a fight.

Rage, not fear, burned hot through her veins.

"In a hurry?" Steroids coughed, closing his arms around her as she kicked and screamed.

This time, she would fight back.

Burly must've drawn his gun. Cold metal pressed to the side of her head, and her arms went limp at the memory of what had happened before.

Give up and they win.

Those bastards wouldn't get the satisfaction. She leaned forward and bit Steroids in the chest as hard as she could.

"Bitch!" He pushed her back a step until she slammed into Burly, whirled her around and tied her hands behind her back.

Sirens grew louder. Thank God, someone had called the police.

Maybe she could stall long enough for the cops to save her?

They dragged her a few steps toward the back door. She made her body go limp.

A blow below her left cheek made her eye feel as if it might pop out of its socket. She spit blood.

Tires squealed out back.

The cops?

No. Couldn't be. There'd be sirens.

Realization crashed down on her, squeezing her lungs. Her heart sank.

The getaway vehicle had just arrived.

Let them take her out of that market, and she may as well be dead.

Sadie kicked and screamed, but they hauled her hands tighter and kept dragging her.

Steroids stuffed a piece of cloth in her mouth, muffling her cries.

Tears burned down her cheeks as fury detonated inside her.

Another ten feet and they could take her anywhere they wanted, do anything they wanted to her. The ICU would be a gift this time. She knew with everything inside her if they got her out the door this time, she'd end up in the morgue.

Her body railed against the bindings on her wrists.

Instead of feeling fear, she felt…resolve.

They could take away her body. They could do anything they wanted to her physically. They could end her life and erase her existence. But while she had breath in her lungs, they would not control her mind.

She felt herself being hauled up and tossed into the back of the sport-utility. Burly got in on one side, Steroids the other. There were two men in the front. The one on the passenger's side was bleeding, losing a fair amount of blood. He held a blood-soaked T-shirt to his left-arm triceps.

She memorized every detail of their faces before the two in the backseat forced her onto the floorboard.

If, no *when,* she escaped, she would testify against the whole lot of them. She would ensure these men were locked away forever. They would not hurt another soul.

Moving her jaw back and forth, she was able to get her tongue behind the cloth to force it out of her mouth.

She remembered sticking her cell phone in her right front pocket. Could she get to it without them noticing?

With her hands tied behind her back, it would be challenging. Could she stretch far enough?

Think. Think. Think.

Lying on her left, facing toward the back, pretty much ensured they'd see her trying to reach into her pocket. Maybe she could distract them somehow? Or bait them into rolling her over to her other side.

"You're a bunch of idiots if you think you'll get away with this. A U.S. Marshal is right behind me. He knows who you are. He knows who your boss is. And he'll find me. When he does, you're all going to jail where you belong."

"I don't think so," Burly said.

A glance passed between them that parked a boulder on Sadie's chest. *Oh. God. No.*

Nothing could happen to Nick.

And, yet, she knew he'd have to be shot or dead not to have come after her already. He hadn't made an attempt to reach her. Her cell hadn't vibrated. No one had called her name or ambushed the men who'd abducted her.

Her heart lurched, threatening to lock up and stop beating.

And let those bastards win? She didn't think so.

She had to reach out to someone.

If she was able to palm her cell—and that was a pretty big if—she'd have access to Smith. For a brief moment, she wondered if Smith had put a tracer on her phone. Maybe he was tracking her right now?

A little voice inside her head reminded her that wouldn't happen. Smith would have given them an untraceable phone. He'd been specific about not wanting to know where they were. It was a safeguard. He'd do it to protect them.

She kicked up at Burly, connecting with his shin.

"Dammit," he grumbled. He tied her ankles together, making it impossible to kick again.

She fought back, not because she thought she'd win, but in order to sell switching positions so she could roll on the other side and access her phone.

By the time they finished, she was facing the opposite direction. On her right side, she could hide the fact she was slipping her phone out of her pocket.

Tears pricked the backs of her eyes.

Despair was an ache in her chest. Sorrow for Nick threatened to suck her under like a riptide and spit her out into the deep.

Before she could say another word, the cloth was being jammed into her mouth again. This time, they tied a strip of material around her head to secure her gag.

Sadie couldn't afford tears.

She had to keep herself calm and force herself to believe that Nick was out there, somewhere, making his way back to her.

Every movement hurt. The bindings around her wrists tightened as she tried to angle her hands toward her right front pocket.

With two fingers, she managed to grasp the corner of her cell well enough to slide it free. She scooted forward, managing to block it with her hip. The phone was already set to vibrate mode. She switched to mute, touched the second name on her contact list, Smith, and covered the speaker with her finger, just in case.

"Where are you taking me?" Her words were muffled

by the gag. She knew full well these guys wouldn't hand over the answer easily.

"Someplace no one will hear you when you scream," Burly said.

NICK BLINKED HIS blurry eyes open. Darkness surrounded him. He couldn't quite put his finger on why he had the urge to run. And what the hell was up with the hammering between his temples?

His body ached. His knees jammed into his face. There were hard walls all around him.

Where was he?

He felt around on his head for bumps, located a couple.

Memories flooded him, coming back all at one time, as if someone had unlocked the gates and sprung open both doors.

"Sadie."

He tried to kick. Only managed to thump his lip with his knee when he moved. He was inside some kind of compartment. No signs of light either meant it was nighttime, or the storm still hadn't passed. The place was airtight.

Rocking back and forth, he tried to free his arms.

Thoughts of the gun battle broke through his mind. He'd told Sadie to run. He'd known they were outnumbered, but he'd tried to get the attention on him and allow her to escape.

He knew they were both in trouble when he saw the shooter immediately give chase.

The vegetable bin. He'd made it. Must've hid him long enough for the police to arrive and scare off Jamison and his men.

Nick felt around. He'd wedged himself inside in a position that was impossible to get out of.

There was no escape.

He heard a familiar voice.

Paul?

Shouting to his friend was a risk. Nick couldn't be sure how long he'd been in that box. Could be minutes or hours. The cops could've come and gone, and so could Grimes or Jamison.

Nick listened intently through the pounding in his temples, straining to hear if there were other voices.

A neighbor must've phoned the police after hearing gunfire.

When he was reasonably certain Paul was alone, he shouted.

"Paul," Nick repeated, louder this time. Shouting made everything hurt, and his head feel as if it might explode. He ignored the pain. Sadie was in trouble. He had to get out of this box and find her.

"Paul!"

Nick heard sounds outside.

"Who is that? Who's here?" Paul's voice trembled.

"It's me. Nick. I need your help to get me out of here."

"Nick?" came the trepid response.

"Open the door, Paul. It's me."

Light split what was left of Nick's head. Yet, it was welcomed.

"What the heck happened to you? How'd you end up in my aunt's vegetable bin?"

"What time is it?" Nick asked, trying to muscle his way out of the container.

"Here. Let me help you."

Where was Sadie? "The woman I was with earlier. Where is she?"

"I don't know. She's not here," Paul said, offering a hand up.

Nick took it and, with a push, broke out of the small container he'd forced himself in. He scanned the area.

"The police are out front. They're asking a lot of questions. I told them I don't know what happened. My neighbor called me when he heard the guns. The old guy kind of freaked out. Called the police, too."

"Did they arrest anyone?" If the police were still there, then Sadie couldn't be too far.

"No one here. My neighbor said he saw everybody run. I didn't expect you to be here, either. I jumped when I heard your voice. That's for sure."

"Which way did they go?" He remembered telling Sadie to run, some of his thoughts were still jumbled, and he'd already lost precious time. He didn't want to risk going off in the wrong direction while his brain was still scrambled.

"The old guy said she went this way." Paul inclined his head toward the left.

"Good. Now do me a favor, and go get the police." Nick needed as many hands on this case as he could get. He checked his pockets for his cell.

His legs cramped.

He tried to walk, but they gave.

Paul grabbed Nick's arm in time to keep him from losing balance and landing on the ground.

"You wait right here, my friend. I'll get the police."

"I lost my cell. It might be on the side of your house." He was grateful to be alive, but what about Sadie?

With him out of the picture, they could do whatever they wanted to her.

Maybe she'd escaped?

Not likely. There were too many men. Jamison must've brought everyone to this fight.

Damn, Nick needed his cell. He needed to make contact with Smith.

The thought of anyone hurting Sadie was like an acid burn on his skin.

A uniformed officer approached. "I need to see some ID, sir."

Nick produced his badge and gave a statement.

"Nick," Paul shouted from the other side of the fence. He burst through. "I found it. These belong to you?"

He held out a cell and a gun.

"Looks like mine." His Glock felt right in his hand. He checked his cell. A dozen missed calls from Smith. "I need to check in with my boss."

The officer nodded.

Smith answered immediately.

"Is she alive?" Nick asked.

"Someone activated her cell phone and used it to call me. I believe it was her."

"Any idea where she is?"

"No. I can tell she's in some type of vehicle. She asked the question of where she was being taken and a man replied they were taking her where no one would hear her scream. It was tough to make out her words. Sounded like something was covering her mouth." He paused. "They could be taking her to a field out in the middle of nowhere for all we know. Without GPS on that phone, I can't track her."

Nick's brain immediately kicked into gear. "There's a place I can think of that no one would hear her scream. The warehouse."

The sounds of fingers flying across a keyboard came through Nick's line. "My closest man is a half hour away."

"I can be there in fifteen minutes."

"Nick," Smith said. Nick didn't like the sound of his

voice when he said it. "They've sent word through one of my informants that they've got Lucy."

Nick ground out a curse. "Can you confirm?"

"I spoke to your brother Luke and she hasn't checked in or answered her phone. Doesn't mean they have her. I just can't confirm one way or the other. They're threatening to drop her body off below the Ferris wheel ride in Fair Park."

Nick's knees buckled. The officer held him steady. "I go to Fair Park, and they'll kill me and Sadie. I go to Sadie and they'll kill Lucy."

"If they have her."

Was it a risk he was willing to take? Jamison clearly knew how much Nick loved and protected his family.

"I can send people to either place, or both. It's your call," Smith said quietly.

Could Sadie already be dead? No. They'd use her to bring Nick out. As soon as they got to him, they'd kill her.

His mind clicked through other possibilities. If he went to Lucy, they'd be ready for him. As soon as they got him, they'd kill Sadie.

He had one advantage. "They don't know that I know about the warehouse. That's where they'd take Sadie. I go to Lucy, and we're all dead."

His stomach lining braided. Make the wrong call and two of the people he loved more than anything in the world would be dead.

"Send your people to Fair Park, but have them wait for my word."

"Got it."

Ending the call, Nick locked gazes with the officer. "I need a ride."

The man in uniform was already bolting toward his squad car.

Running sent a wave of nausea rippling through Nick. He ignored it and pressed on. The thought of anyone hurting Sadie or Lucy sent him to a dark mental place.

He forced all thoughts out of his head that he might be too late.

En route, he bandaged his gunshot wound using supplies from the officer's first-aid kit. They'd split his shoulder with a bullet. He packed gauze on it to stem the bleeding, and secured it with tape.

"No chance you'll let me investigate this lead after I drop you off at the hospital?"

"None whatsoever."

"Then I'll have an ambulance waiting a block away."

"No sirens. I don't want to give these scumbags any warning," Nick said.

The officer nodded before calling it in.

With lights blazing, the cop beat the time by two minutes. He'd cut the lights a block away. "I'll take the front entrance."

"You already know this, but these men are armed, and they're not afraid to shoot an officer. Be careful." Nick hopped out of the car before it came to a complete stop.

He moved to the back of the building, fighting the pain and nausea threatening to buckle his knees. There was a beige sport-utility parked in the back of the building.

Crouching low, he made it to the rear of the vehicle. His gun drawn, he raised high enough to see through the dark window. The vehicle was empty. He moved to the side.

Whoever sat on the passenger's side sure lost a lot of blood. The thought this could be Sadie's blood cut through him. He bit back a curse.

Could belong to anyone. Nick had fired quite a few shots at the jerks, he reminded himself.

A thought nearly leveled him.

Was she even here?

He canceled the thought. This was the most logical place to take her. She had to be inside. He would find her and give her life back to her. A life with him? The thought of opening himself up to that kind of potential pain usually almost flattened Nick.

Not when it came to Sadie. She was different.

Yet, no matter how strong Nick's feelings were, he couldn't ask her to spend the rest of her life waiting up nights and wondering if he'd be coming home. She deserved so much more. Could he give her everything?

A piece of him wished he could.

He loved her. And because he did, he planned to give her something she could only have without him. Peace.

The bay door was half-closed, providing an opportunity to slip into the back of the warehouse.

Breeching the building was easy.

Too easy?

Nick might be walking into a trap.

The main floor of the warehouse was empty.

He glanced up a small flight of stairs into the office.

Several men were there.

His heart raced when he saw her. Sadie. She was there. In the upstairs office.

There were too many men for him to take on, even with the officer who was making his way through the front of the building as backup.

Two against five. Grimes was there. As was Jamison. There were three others in the office.

Nick heard a door open to his left. He pressed his back against the wall and eased toward the sound. A bathroom?

Two against six. He liked those odds even less.

Burly walked out, zipping his pants, his gun holstered.

Nick hit him in the back of the head so hard, he knocked Burly unconscious, catching him on the way down.

The move took almost all of Nick's strength.

He leaned against the wall and took a deep breath.

Glancing up, Nick saw the officer moving toward him. The officer inclined his chin, moving silently.

When he approached them, he pulled out handcuffs. Nick hesitated, almost unsure who those were meant for. But the officer went right to work on Burly.

Five to two increased the odds. Sadie was a fighter. Maybe he should count her as a third.

The officer grabbed the scruff of Burly's neck and hauled him outside.

He returned a moment later. "He's not waking up anytime soon," he whispered. "And if he does, he's not going anywhere."

"Good job. And thanks."

"What do you want to do next?"

The correct answer would be to wait for backup. As long as the men in that room gave him time, Nick would take it. They make a move toward Sadie, and game on. "Keep an eye on them until more men arrive."

He motioned the officer to follow him.

They made it up the stairwell without giving away their position.

The sight of a gun aimed at Sadie's head forced Nick's hand.

He burst into the room, hoping like hell they would believe Burly was returning from the restroom. "I'm Marshal Campbell. You're all under arrest."

Catching them off guard gave him the advantage.

Grimes redirected his weapon toward Nick, but he'd already leveled his and fired.

The officer came in behind Nick, weapon raised.

Steroids put his hands in the air, as did the other pair of men in the room.

"You think you can arrest me?" Jamison aimed his weapon at Sadie.

If Nick fired, Jamison might pull the trigger out of reflex.

Sadie would be dead.

She looked up at Nick, and he expected to see fear in her big green eyes, and he did. But he also saw anger and determination. Good. He could work with that.

If she could distract Jamison, Nick could make a move. Could he signal her somehow?

Her gaze was intent on him. He glanced from her to Jamison's knees.

She gave a slight nod. Bent over on all fours, with Jamison standing over her, she dove into his legs.

He buckled. Nick surged toward Jamison, knocking him a couple of steps backward and away from Sadie.

Gunfire split the air as Nick landed on top of his target and wrestled for control of the weapon. Jamison threw a jackhammer of a punch, connecting with Nick's nose. Blood spurted.

Nick counterpunched, his fist slamming into Jamison's jaw.

Jamison bucked and rolled, causing Nick to lose his grip on Jamison's wrist. Nick adjusted, popping to his knees. He squeezed powerful thighs to hold Jamison, facedown, in place.

Blood poured down Nick's shirt as he cuffed the snake.

Shock overtook Nick as he realized the blood was his.

Once Jamison was secure, Nick folded over to the

sounds of officers rushing downstairs. The one who'd breeched the building with him stood over Jamison, his gun aimed at his temple, as Nick rolled over onto his side, fighting the nausea and fatigue gripping him.

Damn.

He was shot? He immediately thought of Sadie. She was safe now.

The next thing he knew, she was over him, tears streaming down her beautiful cheeks.

"Stay with me, Nick," she begged. The desperation in her voice was palpable. Almost enough to force him to come back to her.

She was safe.

What about Lucy?

As the scene in front of him played out in slow motion, he watched officers handcuff the dirtbags. One of them moved to Nick's side and held his cell phone to his ear. "Someone wants to speak to you."

"Nick? It's Lucy. I'm okay."

Relief flooded him. Sadie was safe. Lucy was okay. Nothing else mattered.

All he wanted to do was close his eyes and go to sleep.

Sadie's voice became distant. Her pleas for him to stay awake faded.

Nick closed his eyes and allowed darkness to claim him.

NICK WOKE WITH a start.

He glanced around the stark white room. His vision was blurry. Where was he?

He tried to push up, unwilling to admit the fear creeping through his system, its icy tendrils closing around his heart.

The case was closed, and he'd most likely never see

Sadie again. The thought caused worse pain than the bullet hole in his shoulder. A few stitches, a little physical therapy, and he'd eventually heal from that. Being without Sadie for the rest of his life put a hollow ache in his chest he'd never recover from.

"Nick?" the voice sounded uncertain and afraid.

Sadie?

He forced his eyes to stay open through the burn and glanced around the room. She was already to the side of the bed before his eyes could focus properly.

"How do you feel?" she asked, reaching out to touch his face.

The sight of her quieted his worst fear—the fear he'd never look into those beautiful eyes again and tell her just how much she meant to him.

"Dizzy. Nauseous." *Relieved.*

"You lost a lot of blood when you were shot," she said. "You must be in pain. Let me call the nurse."

Of course, he just realized, he was in the hospital. But he didn't want the nurse. He had everything he needed right next to him. Sadie.

He covered her hand with his, preventing her from pushing the call button. The whole scenario came back to him in a flood. The warehouse. Grimes. Jamison. "How long have I been out?"

"Two days."

"You've been here the whole time?"

Her cheeks flushed as she nodded. "Luke sneaks Boomer in every chance he gets."

"Tell me what happened."

"Grimes is dead. Jamison shot you. They arrested him, and he's going away for a very long time. So are the others in the warehouse. A few more of his men were arrested at Fair Park."

"And Lucy?"

"She's fine. Calls every hour to check on you, though." Her smile warmed his insides.

"And Meg?"

"She had a little boy."

He couldn't stop himself from reaching out and touching her beautiful face. "You've been keeping track of everyone?"

"I knew you'd want to know as soon as you woke up."

"How's Boomer?"

"He's keeping Gran company at the ranch. She texts me pictures of him every hour." She laughed.

"I remember what you did in the warehouse. I'm proud of you." His chest filled with an emotion that felt a hell of a lot like pride.

She leaned into his palm, and then kissed his hand.

"You been here the whole time?"

She nodded. "There's nowhere else I want to be."

He couldn't believe the love of his life was sitting right there. It would be better if they were somewhere else besides the hospital for what he needed to say. He wished they were somewhere romantic. He needed to ask her something, and he wanted everything to be perfect.

He canceled the thought.

Fact was there would never be a better time than now. "I need you to know that I've fallen hard for you."

He was rewarded with a bright smile. She leaned over and pressed a kiss to his lips. He kept her close when he whispered, "I love you."

She kissed him again, with more enthusiasm this time. "I love you, Nick Campbell."

This time, he wouldn't be stupid enough to let Sadie walk out that door without knowing exactly what she meant to him. He had no intention of repeating his past mistakes.

He knew what he wanted for the rest of his life, and he wanted Sadie.

"I'd prefer to do this on one knee, but I'm guessing that would cause a whole host of people to come rushing through that door..."

She gasped, tears streaming down her cheeks.

"I don't have a ring to offer you right now. But I sincerely pray my heart and the promise of forever will be enough. Sadie Brooks, will you marry me?"

The minute she took to answer felt like an eternity.

She nodded through her tears. "Yes. I will marry you, Nick Campbell. I want very much to be your wife."

"And I want to be your protector for the rest of our days."

* * * * *

Barb Han's THE CAMPBELLS OF CREEK BEND
continues next month with GUT INSTINCT.
*Look for it wherever you'd find
Harlequin Intrigue books!*

REQUEST YOUR FREE BOOKS!
2 FREE NOVELS PLUS 2 FREE GIFTS!

H HARLEQUIN®

INTRIGUE®

BREATHTAKING ROMANTIC SUSPENSE

YES! Please send me 2 FREE Harlequin Intrigue® novels and my 2 FREE gifts (gifts are worth about $10). After receiving them, if I don't wish to receive any more books, I can return the shipping statement marked "cancel." If I don't cancel, I will receive 6 brand-new novels every month and be billed just $4.74 per book in the U.S. or $5.24 per book in Canada. That's a savings of at least 14% off the cover price! It's quite a bargain! Shipping and handling is just 50¢ per book in the U.S. and 75¢ per book in Canada.* I understand that accepting the 2 free books and gifts places me under no obligation to buy anything. I can always return a shipment and cancel at any time. Even if I never buy another book, the two free books and gifts are mine to keep forever.

182/382 HDN F42N

Name	(PLEASE PRINT)	
Address		Apt. #
City	State/Prov.	Zip/Postal Code

Signature (if under 18, a parent or guardian must sign)

Mail to the **Harlequin® Reader Service:**
IN U.S.A.: P.O. Box 1867, Buffalo, NY 14240-1867
IN CANADA: P.O. Box 609, Fort Erie, Ontario L2A 5X3
**Are you a subscriber to Harlequin Intrigue books
and want to receive the larger-print edition?
Call 1-800-873-8635 or visit www.ReaderService.com.**

* Terms and prices subject to change without notice. Prices do not include applicable taxes. Sales tax applicable in N.Y. Canadian residents will be charged applicable taxes. Offer not valid in Quebec. This offer is limited to one order per household. Not valid for current subscribers to Harlequin Intrigue books. All orders subject to credit approval. Credit or debit balances in a customer's account(s) may be offset by any other outstanding balance owed by or to the customer. Please allow 4 to 6 weeks for delivery. Offer available while quantities last.

Your Privacy—The Harlequin® Reader Service is committed to protecting your privacy. Our Privacy Policy is available online at www.ReaderService.com or upon request from the Harlequin Reader Service.

We make a portion of our mailing list available to reputable third parties that offer products we believe may interest you. If you prefer that we not exchange your name with third parties, or if you wish to clarify or modify your communication preferences, please visit us at www.ReaderService.com/consumerschoice or write to us at Harlequin Reader Service Preference Service, P.O. Box 9062, Buffalo, NY 14269. Include your complete name and address.

"The woman in Greenleaf Bar was you?"

"You don't remember?"

"Vaguely."

He struggled to put things in perspective. That had been a hell of a night. He'd stopped at the first bar he'd come to after leaving the rodeo. A blonde had sat down next to him. As best he remembered, he'd given her an earful about the rodeo, life and death as he'd become more and more inebriated.

She must have offered him a ride back to his hotel since his truck had still been at the bar when he'd gone looking for it the next morning. If Brit was telling the truth, the woman must have gone into the motel with him and they'd ended up doing the deed.

If so, he'd been a total jerk. She'd been as drunk as him and driven or she'd willingly taken a huge risk.

Hard to imagine the woman staring at him now ever

being that careless or impulsive.

"Is that your normal pattern, Mr. Dalton?" Brit asked. "Use a woman to satisfy your physical needs and then ride off to the next rodeo?"

"That's a little like the armadillo calling the squirrel roadkill, isn't it? I'm sure I didn't coerce you into my bed if I was so drunk I can't remember the experience."

"I can assure you that you're nowhere near that irresistible. I have never been in your bed."

"Whew. That's a relief. I'd have probably died of frostbite."

"This isn't a joking matter."

"I'm well aware. But I'm not the enemy here, so you can quit talking to me like I just climbed out from under a slimy rock. If you're not Kimmie's mother, who is?"

"My twin sister, Sylvie Hamm."

Twin sisters. That explained Brit's attitude. Probably considered her sister a victim of the drunken sex urges he didn't remember. It also explained why Brit Garner looked familiar.

"So why is it I'm not having this conversation with Sylvie?"

"She's dead."

Find out what happens next in
MIDNIGHT RIDER
by Joanna Wayne,
available January 2015 wherever
Harlequin Intrigue® books and ebooks are sold.

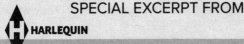
"We've got to get you out of here."

"I am not helpless, Pete. I've been in self-defense courses my entire life. And I know how to shoot. My gun's in the bag we left outside."

Good to know, but he wasn't letting her near that bag. He dropped the key ring on the floor near her hands. "Find one that looks like it's to a regular inside door. Like a broom closet. I'm going to lock you inside."

"Are you sure they're still out there?"

"The chopper's on the ground. The blades are still rotating. No telling how many were already here ready to ambush us." He watched two shadows cross the patio. "Let's move. Next to the snack bar, there's a maintenance door. Run. I'll lay down cover if we need it."

They ran. He could see the shadows but no one followed. Hopefully they didn't have eyes on him or Andrea. He heard the keys and a couple of curses behind him, then a door swung open enough for his charge to squeeze through.

He saw the glint of sun off a mirror outside. They were watching.

"Can you lock the door? Will it lock without the key?"

"I think so."

"Keep the keys with you. I don't need them. Less risky." Bullets could work as a key to unlock, but they might not risk injuring Andrea. He was counting on that.

"But, Pete—"

"Let me do my job, Andrea. Once you're inside, see if you can get into the crawl space. They just saw you open the door. Hide till the cavalry arrives."

"You mean the navy. He won't let us down," she said from the other side of the door. "This is his thing, after all."

Pete had done all he could do to hide her. Now he needed to protect her.

Find out what happens next in
THE SHERIFF
by Angi Morgan,
available January 2015 wherever
Harlequin Intrigue® books and ebooks are sold.

HIEXP69808

HARLEQUIN®

A *Romance* FOR EVERY MOOD™

Love the Harlequin book you just read?

Your opinion matters.

Review this book on your favorite book site, review site, blog or your own social media properties and share your opinion with other readers!

Be sure to connect with us at:
Harlequin.com/Newsletters
Facebook.com/HarlequinBooks
Twitter.com/HarlequinBooks

HARLEQUIN®

A *Romance* FOR EVERY MOOD™

JUST CAN'T GET ENOUGH?

Join our social communities
and talk to us online.

You will have access to the latest
news on upcoming titles and special
promotions, but most importantly,
you can talk to other fans about your
favorite Harlequin reads.

Harlequin.com/Community

 Facebook.com/HarlequinBooks

Twitter.com/HarlequinBooks

Pinterest.com/HarlequinBooks